AT MIDNIGHT ON THE 31ST OF MARCH

New York Classics

FRANK BERGMANN, SERIES EDITOR

At Midnight
ON THE 31ST OF MARCH

JOSEPHINE YOUNG CASE

Foreword by
FRANK BERGMANN

SYRACUSE UNIVERSITY PRESS

Syracuse University Press Edition 1990
99 98 97 96 95 94 93 92 91 90   6 5 4 3 2 1

Originally published by Houghton Mifflin Company, The Riverside Press Cambridge.

Publication of this book was made possible through the assistance of Colgate University, St. Lawrence University, and Skidmore College.

FRONTISPIECE BY EDWIN EARLE

The paper used in this publication meets the minimum requirements of American National Standard for Information Sciences—Permanence of Paper for Printed Library Materials, ANSI Z39.48–1984. ∞™

Library of Congress Cataloging-in-Publication Data

Case, Josephine Young, 1907–
    At midnight on the 31st of March / Josephine Young Case ; foreword by Frank Bergmann.
        p.   cm.
    "Originally published [1938] by Houghton Mifflin Company, the Riverside Press, Cambridge."
    ISBN 0-8156-2492-1 (alk. paper)
    I. Title.
PS3505.A819A8   1990
811'.52—dc20   89-26180
                                                        CIP

MANUFACTURED IN THE UNITED STATES OF AMERICA

To

IDA BRANDOW YOUNG

who would have known what to do

JOSEPHINE YOUNG CASE, a longtime resident of upstate New York, has a record of achievement that is hard to match. Refusing to choose between marriage and a career, she resolved to have both—and did so successfully. She has served as acting president of Skidmore College, as director of Bryn Mawr, and on numerous national committees, including President Johnson's Advisory Committee on Foreign Assistance. Following *At Midnight* (1938), she wrote a historical novel, *Written in Sand* (1945), a book of poems, *Freedom's Farm* (1946), a short prose narrative, *This Very Tree* (1969), and coauthored with her husband, Everett Case, a biography of her father, *Owen D. Young and American Enterprise* (1982).

FOREWORD

JOSEPHINE YOUNG CASE had a great idea. "I'll never get such a good idea again," she wrote in her diary. The resulting book, *At Midnight on the 31st of March*, first published in 1938, the same year as Thornton Wilder's *Our Town*, with which it has a great deal in common, is here brought back into print in the New York Classics series.

It was the author's own home village of Van Hornesville, New York, thinly disguised as Saugersville in this remarkable blank verse narrative, and the surrounding countryside between Fort Plain on the Mohawk and Richfield Springs on the old Western Turnpike (U.S. Route 20) that served as a setting for this poem. In Case's story, at midnight on that last day of March, the lights suddenly go out, the telephone is dead, "the road ain't there no more." Search parties report that civilization, human life, is nowhere to be found but in their own small village of Saugersville.

The townspeople are forced to sort themselves out. Hopes are dashed, dependencies smashed, relations redrawn. This is a study of Emersonian self-reliance in exigency, tempered by people's need to function as a community nevertheless. What is hidden in their hearts is either refined out of existence or forced into eruption. In a year of hardship, individual resourcefulness and communal interdependence are rediscovered; the meaning of human life—through dramatic instances of courtship, marriage, childbirth, and death—is clarified and reaffirmed.

The following March 31st finds the villagers wondering if the lights will come back on, but Case does not tell. She does say that the people "have come closer to the heart of things" and that they are "more able to take hold of life, and joy." Blending back into nature's cycle, the villagers learn how to turn to their deeper advantage the sudden disappearance of mechanical progress.

Edgar Allan Poe would have loved Case's originality. J. R. R. Tolkien would have applauded her example of what he himself termed "recovery," the "regaining of a clear view." The *Saturday Review of Literature* commented that "in detail, in understanding of the people, in atmosphere and background, Mrs. Case has created an authentic picture, full of the strength and weakness of humanity, and true to locality." The award-winning science fiction and fantasy writer Gene Wolfe remarks that "if ever (as I hope) I find myself in Saugersville, ancient or modern, on March 30th, I will stay over for a day and two nights at least."

For my part, I could not put the book down until I had finished it; I found it deeply moving and at times breathtaking reading. The author's blank verse ennobles the search for basic human values, and in America at least a miller is as good as a monarch. Case continues a strong New England tradition of narrative verse, reaching from Michael Wigglesworth's Puritan *The Day of Doom* to Longfellow to Robinson and Frost. The high seriousness of the verse form at all times reminds the reader of the high seriousness of the occasion—and what could be more serious than life and death, love and hate? *At Midnight on the 31st of March* is a jest such as the Bard might make on these foolish mortals; it is everyone's "our town" in poetry.

Josephine Young Case was born on February 16, 1907, in Lexington, Massachusetts, the daughter of Josephine Edmonds and Owen D. Young, the future chairman of General Electric. She was educated at Bryn Mawr (B.A. 1928) and Radcliffe (M.A. 1934), and in 1931 married Everett Needham Case, her father's assistant and later for many years president of Colgate University. Later, she herself was a trustee of Bryn Mawr and of Skidmore College; she served on many high-level national committees and received a number of honorary degrees and other awards. Despite this rich academic life, she remained deeply attached to the rural life and neighbors that she had known since her childhood in Van Hornesville.

At Midnight was Josephine Young Case's first but not her only book. Just as it has one of its roots in the straitened circumstances that the Great Depression imposed on everyone, so World War II gave impetus to her novel *Written in Sand* (1945), a chronicle of William Eaton in the Barbary Wars of 1805 with an under-

ix

lying connection to the American campaign in North Africa nearly one-hundred-fifty years later. A volume of diverse poems, *Freedom's Farm*, appeared in 1946; it is informed by her classical training, her love of the country, and the just-concluded war. There followed a short prose narrative, *This Very Tree*, in 1969. For lack of a better term, I will call it a college novel, of which genre it is quite the deepest and wisest exemplar I have read. It describes the *ethos* of a college in both classical and native terms; Hesiod's *Works and Days* and the old Indian hemlock above campus represent the natural and intellectual dimensions of education. Finally, she wrote, with Everett Needham Case as coauthor, *Owen D. Young and American Enterprise: A Biography* (1982), which, considering the paucity of literature on her own life and work, says less about Josephine Young Case than one wishes, though it richly informs the reader about the Van Hornesville family roots. *At Midnight* itself is dedicated to Owen's mother, "who would have known what to do."

I am grateful to Everett Case for sharing information, recollections, and above all a sense of Josephine Young Case's abiding humanity.

Frank Bergmann

Utica College of Syracuse University
September 1989

x

AT MIDNIGHT ON THE 31ST OF MARCH

AT

MIDNIGHT

ON THE THIRTY-FIRST OF MARCH

I

☆

I

AT MIDNIGHT on the thirty-first of March
No light shone out upon the village street
And every head in all of Saugersville
Was laid upon its pillow, sleep or wake.
Patches of white, the last of winter's snow,
Collected all the little light there was
Under a cloudy sky, between dark hills,
To shine alone of all things visible.
Only the slippery road, the roaring creek,
Two dozen houses in a valley cleft,
A mill, a store, two steeples pointing up,
A school, garage, the hotel, and the grange
Were Saugersville, for anyone to see,
Given light to see by, or an eye to see.

Back upon the hill a restless head,
Too hot upon the pillow, called for light,
And restless hands reached for the switch; the bulb
As quick and brilliant as a lightning flash
Answered obedient and set forth the scene.

(1)

Tortured by solitude, and thought, and pain,
The young man's face shone bright before the lamp,
And homesick eyes looked straight into its light
As though it were his friend, a modern friend,
An urban banner in a rural land.
Desiring always what his health forbade —
The city's life and all the city's ways,
Which had been always his, until disease
Had sent him out to lead another life
Close to the earth, in sunshine and the air:
A lonely life, alone upon the hill;
A garden, and his house, and in it books,
Books always — now he turned again to read,
Seeking forever in philosophy
The answers he had sought for in his life
And nothing in his life had helped to find.

The sentences went on and on; his mind
Only half knew what moved before his eyes.
He rubbed his head and thought, 'This light's not
      good.'
And now indeed the bulb was not so bright
And faded every second, till it seemed
Almost a candle in the shadowy room.
Entranced, he watched it fade until a glow,
A gleaming end as on a candlewick,
Shone, and went out, and dark swept all around.
Lighting a match, he found another bulb
And screwed it in, but this too gave no light.

Stepping across the room, familiar, quick,
He found the switch that lit the kitchen light;
It clicked, and dark remained. The power was
        off.
He cursed the company and went to bed.

April the first was grey, a smoky dawn
That lifted sullenly behind the hill.
The air smelled strange. Muttering to himself,
Ed Winterhaus went slowly to the barn.
'There'll be a storm today or I'm a liar.'
The barn was dark inside, the cows smelled sweet.
He went to switch the light on, get to work, —
Even with machines there's work to do to milk.
No lights answered the switch his careless hand
Turned with a habit that required no thought.
But thought flashed on when no lights came to
        life.
He tried again; no answer. And the switch
That worked the milk machine was also dead.
He scratched his head, then tried what little ways
He knew to fix the thing, but soon found out
There was no power, nor any to be had.
He went to get a lantern, call his wife,
And saw the kitchen lit by kerosene —
A dusty lamp that stood upon the shelf
These fifteen years. — He shook his head and called,
'Come on Maria get to work. The cows
Will get a taste of oldtime milking now.'

(3)

By eight o'clock the farmer's milk is down
And teams and trucks and cars have brought their cans
To load on George's truck which, red and big,
Travels the thirteen miles to Centerfield,
The creamery and railroad. George is gone
By eight-fifteen, and everybody comes
To market at the store, to get the mail,
And talk about the government or the weather.
Upon that Monday morning, April first,
There was no talk except about the power,
And anger, curiosity, and spleen,
Varied in talk with well-contented words
From those, too poor or too conservative,
That had no electricity in their homes.
At last Earl Backus said — a man so slow
To move one would not guess the agile brain
Behind the grey and angled face — 'Say, Bert,
Why don't you call the company and ask
What kind of service they are giving us?'
Bert Snyder, merchant general, a man
Little and sharp and kind, went to the phone
While all the group around the stove said, 'Yes
That's what we'll do, call up the company
And ask them what the hell.' Bert turned the crank
And listened. Now outside the store the grey
Reluctant morning lightened up to show
The concrete road that ran straight through the town
White and untravelled. Everything was still
But for the few and quiet calls and cries

(4)

Of children walking down the road to school.
Bert rang again, and anxious rang once more,
While silence dropped around the stove and all
Listened as still as he. At last he turned
And puzzled said, 'Don't get no answer here.
The line seems dead. There must be something wrong.'

There were no curses now, but baffled looks
And words on every lip that tried to find
The answer. 'If there'd been a storm, or snow
To break the poles and wires, that'd be one thing,
But wind ain't blowed and water ain't so high
It could do damage. Last year when the flood
Was down the valley, lights and phone were good.'

Now George came in, that drove the big red truck,
An hour before his time, and crossed the room
To warm his hands before the stove that showed
Such scarlet warmth in little window panes.
Bert went to say, 'Why, George, you here?' — and
        stopped
Because he saw his face. And all were still
And said no word, but looked at him and waited.
He was a burly man, and handsome too,
As easy-going as they come, and good,
But hated work, and found his big red truck
Better companion than a plow or hoe.
I don't suppose he ever had a thought
Except of what was standing right in front of him.

You wouldn't say he had much mind to lose,
But now he looked like all he had was gone.
They waited, and it might have been an hour
Before he spoke. 'The road ain't there no more.'
He sat down in a chair that creaked, and none
Replied. His hands that hung between his knees
Were shaking and his face was grey. He said,
'The mist hung down the valley, so I drove
Real slow. I couldn't hardly see my way
Down through Green Hollow. And the road seemed
       rough.
There round that biggest curve 'twas awful rough,
And then — there wasn't any road at all.
The bridge, the concrete bridge down just beyond —
Well, I could see it wasn't there. And then
I had to back — I couldn't turn — and backed
A half a mile, and came here quick's I could.'

No one said much, but finally Earl got up
And slowly went to get his car, and more
Went after, till a cavalcade of cars
Moved down the road as fast as they could go.
All went but Bert, who had to mind the store
Come Judgement Day.

Ede Salzenbach, who lived across the way,
Had seen the men come out and go. She ran
To ask Mis' Snyder what the trouble was,
And soon a little group of puzzled wives

Stood looking down the road. Was this new thing
Another aberration of the men,
More serious, but still a male defect?
Or was it really some unheard-of fate,
That meant — as all catastrophe must mean —
More to the women than the men, who must
Bear their own sorrow and their men-folks too?
With sharp uncertain eyes they watched the road
While fear moved in their hearts and chilled their hands.

Over the dinner — for a man must eat
Even though the earth is rolling out from under —
The Warder family talked so fast their mouths
Could hardly keep up with both words and food.
Gus Warder had been one of those to go
To see the road that was no more a road.
'And then we went the other roads besides,
And everyone was just the same as that.
The road up Beeman's hill was good as far
As Ed's back field, and then it disappeared,
Ran out to nothing in a stand of woods
Where there haven't been no woods since I been here.
The western road goes by Abe Givets' place
To where it drops down in that marshy field —
The cat-tails grew right where the gravel was.'
Ma Warder and the pair of little boys
Were thick with questions, but the daughter May
Said nothing and her eyes were full and bright
As though she saw a vision in this thing.

Taking the dishes to the sink Ma paused
To try the switch again. Gus shook his head.
'That's no use. For all the wires are gone.
Down by the bridge they just plain stop.
I couldn't see a sign of those big poles
Of the high-tension line; and great big trees
Are growing where their clearing used to go.'

Taking the car as far as possible
Earl Backus and his brother John and Gus
Went out that afternoon to get to town,
Eight miles beyond the place the road had stopped
Down in Green Hollow. It was late at night
When weary-footed they came back at last
To a village that burned lamps and candles now
Later than electricity before.
Too tired to tell more than the barest tale,
They said they got there — a heart-breaking task
Through woods as thick as jungle, so at last
They tried the stream bed and made better time.
They saw no sign of any human thing.
But deer were there, and once a startled bear
That crashed back through the brush as suddenly
As he had come. And when they found at last
The place the Sauger Creek runs in the river
Where Centerfield had stood two hundred years
There was no town. The still and mighty trees
Loomed by the water where the railroad tracks
Were noisy day and night beside the town.

The current ran on slow and seeming still
A broad and quiet surface, mirrored grey.
Beyond that unbridged width the wooded hills
Stood back against the sky and showed no sign.

II

After another day of futile search
By parties that set out south, east, and west,
And found the very same as on the north —
The endless woods, the silent hills, the streams
Unchecked, unbridged, and nowhere any house
Or any sign of man, there now or ever,
Not anything at all but deer — Roy Smith,
Who went armed with his gun, had shot a buck
And dragged it to the road. He grinned and said,
'If everything is gone I guess the law
Ain't stuck around to bother me for this.'

After these weary men, by twos and threes,
Had come back home, to look with puzzled eyes
Along the roads that were no longer roads,
They asked each other with particular stare
If one and all were raving lunatics,
Or if indeed there was no Centerfield,
No Schuylers Falls, no Indiantown, no Springs,
No state, no city, no America,
But only Saugersville in all the world.

(9)

They held a meeting in the school that night,
And every living soul in Saugersville
That could get up upon two legs was there.
Old Grandma Smith, that laid abed so long
She said she was like to stick, got up and dressed
And hobbled to the school, with every step
Calling a murrain on these lying mouths
That said such foolish things. And Dick Van Snell,
That had two legs, but one of wood and wire,
Walked all the way to tell the company
How rough the road before his place was now.
The children scampered in the vestibule;
The babies cried and sucked and slept again.
Bert Snyder put more wood into the stove
Until it glowed and everybody steamed.
When every soul was there, and talk ran on
Now low and slow, now high-hysterical,
Earl Backus rose and knocked on teacher's desk.
'We'd better talk it over one by one
So all can hear. I will begin and state
That by some chance we cannot understand
The rest of the world has changed, though Saugers-
        ville
Is much the same as ever. Sunday last
I went to Schuylers Falls, and others here
Were different places in the country round
And all was just as we're accustomed to.
But Monday morning things were not the same.
The power was off, the roads were gone, the phone

Was dead, as all of you here know yourselves.
What has come over us, or what has come
To everybody else but us, is more
Than I can even start to understand.'
He paused. 'Before we talk we'd better have
A prayer from Reverend Yule.' The old man rose;
But ten years back he had come here to take
The little church whose few parishioners
Were still enough to keep a minister,
Although the other church was always dark.
A quiet humdrum man, that did his work
Like anyone, and spoke but once a week —
Or so it seemed. But now his eyes were fire.
He opened out his hands and spoke to God.
'Our Father, that looks down upon us now,
That made the world, and doomed it once in rain
Except for Noah and his Ark of life,
That opened up the sea for Israel,
Now by thy will another fate has come
Upon thy people, who look up for aid
Now to our hills, beyond our hills to thee.
Whatever be this thing has come to us,
Guide us to do thy will, who sent a dove
To Noah in the endless sea, and then
Another dove upon thy Son to show
Who came to save us. For his sake we ask
Thy blessing on thy troubled people, Lord.'
And every trembling mouth said low 'Amen.'

Earl Backus said, 'Let's see if we can tell
Just how this came. Can anybody say?'
The young man in the solitary house,
John Herbert, rose and said, 'On Sunday night
I couldn't sleep, and lit the light to read.
I saw the bulb go out; it faded out
As though the power went off by slow degrees.'
Gus Warder said, 'What time would that have been?'
'About eleven ten I took my book
And read almost an hour — midnight, I guess.'
Backus from the teacher's desk went on,
'We've been to Centerfield, and Indiantown,
As far as Sulphur Springs — it's all the same,
No towns at all, not any house or road.
Only the river and the creeks are there
Of all the land and villages we knew.
On Indian Hill Roy Smith climbed up a tree.
You know how all the country lies spread out
From that hilltop. You used to see the smoke
Of half a dozen towns, from engines too,
And sometimes hear the whistle of the train.
You tell 'em, Roy, just how it looked to you.'
The young and silent hunter stiffly rose,
More frightened now to hear himself speak out
Than at that moment in the pine tree top.
'I saw just trees,' he said, 'trees all the way.'

Now Robert Munn, that owned the small garage
And tinkered all the cars and trucks, spoke up.

'I connected up my radio last night
With batteries, and listened in, and tried
Out all the tricks I know. 'Twas half-past eight
When lots is on the air, or used to be.
I couldn't get a sound. I heard the static
Crack and break. Of anything at all
But that there wasn't even the faintest sound.'
Ede Salzenbach got up and shouted out —
A voice like Doomsday trumpet any day
And now more strident than it ever was —
'What's come to everyone? And where are they
Except for us? And what will come to us?
Maybe tomorrow there'll be only trees
In Saugersville. And where will we be then?'
Earl Backus rapped upon the desk and said,
'There's all of us got friends in other towns
Out in that world which doesn't seem to be,
And some have got relations too, and yet ——'
He paused and looked around, and everyone
Looked here and there and counted families
And for a space said nothing. There was Gert,
Ed Winterhaus's girl that went to school
In River City to the Normal School, —
She had come home because she had a cold
And needed rest and sleep and country air.
There were Bill and Mabel Countryman,
Who went to fetch his mother from the town
Where she lived in winter, being cold
On Beeman's hill, and Sunday brought her back.

And everyone was there that really lived
In Saugersville, and no one that did not.
Relations to be sure and many a friend
Were lost along with all the vanished world,
But families for the most were all intact —
'We're mostly here, us that have always lived
Here in this town and made our living here.
Barring some kind of fate that's after us
And hasn't quite caught up, we're going to live
Here in this town awhile. The trouble is
To find just how we're going to do it now.'

And then a silence wavered in the room
As thoughts went tumbling on in every head,
So much to need, so much to puzzle out,
And over all the cloud of secret fate.
For once these human beings saw and felt
Catastrophe on others could be worse
Than on themselves. Now being left alone
When everyone was gone, they almost wished
They too had disappeared; a common fate
Seemed better than survival all alone.
The faces, set or working, stared in space.
Ma Warder cried into her handkerchief; but May
Looked secretly to where John Herbert sat
And thought, 'The city cannot get him now.'

Old Grandma Smith thumped down her heavy stick
And said right out, 'A passel here of fools!

I'm going down to Centerfield to live.'
The men were silent, till Abe Givets spoke.
'Got a tarnation lot of milk to home,
We'll all be throwing milk away, for calves
And pigs and people, butter or cheese,
Won't take it all.' Ed Winterhaus replied,
'We'll likely have to eat the cows and then
Keep just enough for what we need ourselves
For milk and cream and butter, veal and beef.
And pigs — we'd better breed a lot, and hens,
Each one will have to see he's got enough.'
Earl Backus spoke again: 'We're luckier 'n hell
That this is spring. We'll plan to plant the stuff
We need for food and fodder for the year.
We must count all the things we have to have
That used to come from otherwheres and see
Just how we can replace them for ourselves.
There's gasoline' — he looked at Robert Munn.
'I've got twelve hundred gallons in my tanks.
The truck came Saturday.' He paused and thought
How Bill the driver had gone on so fast,
So confident and loud, his heavy wheels
Thundering out of Saugersville — to where?
'I've kerosene, and oil, enough to last
An ordinary month or month and a half.
Of course there isn't any road to go
Except right here, a mile or two and back,
But there's the farm machinery to run.'
Earl Backus frowned. 'It looks to me, my friends,

As though we'll have to have as they did once
A Committee of Safety — five or seven men
To tell us what to do and when to do it.
If you agree let's settle that right now.'

Under the stars that looked so far away,
Blown by a fierce spring wind that whacked the trees,
The people hurried home to light their lamps.
Walking with new responsibility
And courage that even now did not desert,
The elected members of the Safety Board —
Gus Warder, William Countryman, young Smith,
Bert Snyder, and Earl Backus as the head —
Went home as well, to bed if not to sleep.

III

When Maria Winterhaus came down to make
The cookstove fire, she crumpled paper up
Half seeing print, *The Schuylers Falls Tribune*,
And news of happenings in another world
Now gone as it was gone. She stopped halfway,
Smoothed out the paper, folded it, and put
It safe away. With care she laid the fire
Of little sticks that lighted to one match
And even that one she looked at longingly
And shut the matchbox lid with firm despair
The coffee can was full; she put it by,

And heated milk, then made her buckwheat cakes.
The sausage, syrup, butter, bread, and jam
Went on the table with celerity.
She nodded as she set each plate down hard
As though to say, 'At least all these are mine.'
Her daughter Gert, still sniffling in her nose,
Although the excitement had most cured the cold
That brought her home to Saugersville and life,
Stood at the door, her pretty, sleepy face
All discontented at the thought of milk
Instead of coffee; shook her head at Ma
Who brought her buckwheat cakes. 'You know I won't
Eat cakes and get all fat. I'll make some toast.'
Her mother's face was filled with secret joy,
For this catastrophe had brought her home
To keep the presence which she wanted most.
'No need to talk that way. Your stylish friends
In River City won't be caring now
If you are fat or thin. We've got to live
For just ourselves. We might as well be happy.'
The girl said nothing, for her thoughts were dark.
To leave the little village all her life
Had been her deep desire. This year at last
She had succeeded, and begrudged the time
She must be home. She saw a future bright
Though vague awaiting her, the one thing sure
That it would be not here but in the city.
She shrugged and listened to her mother's voice.
'Not but what you've got friends here, you know.

You've always treated young Roy Smith real mean,
The nicest boy of anywheres around.'
'Oh mother leave me be. I've got to live
Now here with you whatever sort of life
We're going to have now all the worth-while things
Are gone. Don't pester me; I'll do my best.
I don't know how I'll stand it but I will.'

The Safety Board met in the school at nine
When chores were done — by puzzled men who tried
To disentangle in their complex scene
What things were really theirs and what had come
From far away and now would come no more.
The quickest survey left them all appalled,
And set within them hard the will to live
As well as may be upon what they had.
The problem first was to look to their food,
For nothing yet nor for some months to come
Could grow in gardens or the sodden fields.
'There's milk enough for twenty towns, and cream,
And we'll be making butter and what cheese
We can. Meat too we'll have in plenty now
With cows to kill — there won't be feed enough
For many head. We'll need our horses most,
And must take care of them and breed them too.
I guess the hardest thing will be the flour.
There'll be some in the mill, and grain to grind —
We can't spare much of that, we need the seed —
But bread will likely be some scarce by fall.

We must plant wheat, we must plant corn for us,
Not only for the stock, potatoes too ——'
Gus Warder stopped, his eyes alight with plans,
As though he saw the fertile fields all green
And bearing for the village sustenance.
'We'd better make a list,' Earl Backus said,
'Of everyone in town. We've got to know
How many mouths there are to feed, and what
They have already. Then we must decide
Just how to portion out our food and goods.
The stuff belongs of course to different ones,
You've got the food right in your store there, Bert,
And Robert has the oil and gas, while Jake
Has all the grain and flour down in the mill,
And others of us have got other things.
You, Bill, have got the beer in your hotel,
And I've a little honey from my hive.
The only market for the stuff we have
Is now right here, where people need it more
Than ever before. We must see what is best
And how we can be fair to everyone.'
They shook their heads and set their minds to work,
More thinking needed than in all their days
Summed up together. Fear and love of life
Worked in them strongly; some sort of justice too
Held back the greed that could not help but burn.

IV

May Warder, standing at the woodhouse door
To rest her arms from churning, smelled the air
That came so sweetly from the melting fields,
The banks where water ran between the grass,
The furrows where the ice of winter ran,
And felt spring in her heart, and looked away
To where the far and wooded hills were blue
Above the brown snow-spotted slopes nearby.
Across the valley, on the northern hill,
Above the road that windingly went down
Deep in the valley to the little town,
She saw the smoke that showed the chimney set
Among the apple trees — John Herbert's house,
Where she had looked in longing more than once.
She drew deep breaths, and saw beyond the smoke
The hill rise up, the barrier to the north
Beyond which lay the wilderness, unknown.
Deep in her breast and spreading through her body
She felt fierce love for home, for this small place
That had been always home. Today it seemed
No narrower than before, for here was all:
The farm, the house, the hills and fields of home,
The family warm beneath the sagging roof.
Yes here is all her lips were saying soft,
Her eyes upon the smoke between the trees.

Jake Cramer shut the doors of his garage
That leaned against the mill, a modern growth
Upon that century-old and sturdy stone.
Behind the doors he still could see the shine
Of paint and chromium, his new sedan;
So hardly bought, so dearly loved, and now
No more than junk, a useless thing, a wreck.
The gas had been apportioned out, to those
Who needed it for farm machinery,
A little left, reserved, in case of need.
What flour and grain Jake had had in the mill
Were all divided up by high fiat,
And written down most carefully in the books
Against the day when cash might be some use.
Jake and Bert and Robert Munn as well
Were promised wood and milk and meat and eggs
From each that got his share, to pay in part
The debt that stood against him in the books.
Jake went to grind, blessing the ancient wheel
That turned the stones so faithfully still for him
Though but this year he had been plotting how
A gasoline engine might do better work,
And in the dust of milling he forgot
To grieve again about the new sedan.

Looking down in the entangled swamp
Where once the road ran hard to Indiantown,
Abe Givets swore and wrinkled up his eyes
And pulled his mouth down sideways so his face

Looked tough and furrowed as a butternut.
The outside world had not been much to Abe,
And Indiantown was just a place to drink,
But this high-handed wholesale wiping out
Of all he knew beyond the narrow hills
Was like a blow directed just to him,
A sharp affront to one who knew his rights.
He kicked the ground and Red, his feeble hound,
Ran sideways in the swamp as though he felt
That cruel toe between his ribs again.
'Those birds that call themselves the Safety Board
Have passelled out a niggling bit of food.
I'll bet they've got a plenty for themselves.
They said each man should keep his money fast
And so I will. There'll be a time some day
That some of them'll be glad to see my cash.
You can't cut money out, for them that has
Are going to have, no matter what they say.'
He shook his fist and kicked the ground again,
And hunched into himself went home to find
The family which with blows he called his own.

The men went homeward in the dusk, their deer
Slung up on poles, their faces looking down
Silent and eager to the valley cleft,
Because they feared that in this day it too
Might be a wilderness and they alone,
An even smaller band left here to face
In twos and threes a strange and hostile world.

The reassuring shine of roof and wall
Broke down their silence and they laughed and said
How sweet the meat would taste, how fine the skin.
But when John Backus asked how many shot
Each man had here, or home, and said how much
Was in the store, the silence fell again.
'I'll make myself a bow of hickory.
I know that I could hit a deer,' said Roy.
'They're pretty tame. I hit a squirrel once
When I was a kid. It was a lucky chance.
But arrows tipped with steel would kill a deer.
The Indians did it once. I guess I can.'

John Herbert dug his garden deep and wide
And planted all the seeds that he could get.
The sun was hot upon his bended back,
The earth was sweet with promise for his seeds.
Making the little furrows as he went,
He thought, 'There'd be more worry and less fun
Making a garden, for a family man.
I should be glad I've got no mouths to feed
But just my own — that's big but only one.'
He straightened up to look beyond the hills
Where lay more hills that climbed up to the sky.
Across the valley now he saw the team
And Gus behind them, plowing up the lot
That lay between the wood-piece and the road
And had been pasture for these many years.
He thought how still the valley looked, how sane.

'I really must be going back to town.
I haven't seen the city for two months.'
And then, 'It can't be true. I know it is a dream.
Tonight I'll waken in the dark and hear
Far on the wind the whistle of a train.'

Ed Winterhaus was not much used to thought
Except for crops and cattle, which he loved.
But he was thinking while his busy fork
Spread out manure to make the garden grow
'I been here all my life; it's fifty years
And then some more, since I was born right there.
I haven't been away from here, but once
To go to the Fair — that's twenty years ago —
Except for trips to Schuylers Falls and such.
I ain't never hankered after going away.
It seemed to me that I belonged right here
And might not fit in other people's towns.
And now I can't go away. There's some I guess
Will be real anxious when they know they can't
And pine to go. Now I don't feel that way.
It's going to mean a lot of work to live
And lots to do without, but that's all right;
I've got the farm, and all the family here,
And living's always work. And when it's done
I'll think of lying there where I can see
My father's stone shine white upon the hill,
Just as I've always thought.   There's not much
          change.'

The Reverend Yule on Sundays found his church
Full to the doors; not only absent ones
From his own congregation but as well
The Methodists and Universalists,
And some that never saw a church before
On the inside, that came so strangely in.
Fired by the faces looking up at him
The old man preached repentance like a John
Crying in this new wilderness. He prayed
Until his hearers trembled at his voice.
'Think not,' he cried, 'you have been singled out
By special virtue for this special fate.
Say not you are the sons of Abraham;
God could make better ones of stones than you.
For very sin you may have been allowed
To live your lives and have another chance,
And you must show that you are worthy now.'
The feeble organ had a trumpet sound,
With earnest feet Miss Elkins pedalled hard
And drew a swelling peal that urged the tune,
'Oh God our help in ages past.'

Abe Givets' wife was only half as old,
A good deal less than half as mean as he.
One of too many children in a crowded house,
At seventeen she had been given to him,
Her father wanting one less mouth to feed.
Thinking to be a woman she was willing,
And proud to have a house to call her own

(25)

Until she found not even her soul was that
And she was less a woman than a slave.
The babies came too fast, but were her own,
Something to love, to nourish and keep warm,
At least until they reached an age to work,
An age which they reached young in Givets' house.
Sometimes when Abe was out in distant fields
She took the children and in breathless haste
Went down the steep three quarters of a mile
To the village and the store — to life.
She had no money, but could spend her eyes
Upon the few bright things Bert Snyder had:
The rolls of printed calico, their flowers
As lovely to her as Chinese brocade;
The ribbons in the case, the greeting cards,
Even the soap that smelled as sweet as flowers.
Set in the narrow circle of her face
Her eyes were big as rabbits' and as soft.
She looked a bigger child among her own,
As tender, pitiful, and ignorant.
To everyone she saw she said a word
Eager and low, that dared not speak at home.
And few thought twice of her except to say,
'She has no easy life that girl I bet.'
Sometimes big George would stop and say hello,
And once he took them in his big red truck
As near to home as she had dared to go
Lest Abe should spy them and get out his strap.
She did not think at all of George except

That here was someone kind who laughed and joked.
But he looked sideways at the childish face
And laughed a little louder at the joke.
George had a wife, but where he did not know,
For tired of boyish tricks and lazy ways
She had been gone two years or more and he
Lived as he could, alone and at his ease.
But now the darling of his life, his truck,
Stood useless in the barn. No more it went
To Centerfield and back with rattling cans;
And now no more those other jaunts by night,
The truck as faithful as a handsomer steed
And girls as pleased to ride in it, with George.
For most a week George had been nearly dumb
After that day he found the road was gone.
But such profound amazement did not serve
To keep him still for long. His loud guffaw
Was heard again about Bert Snyder's stove.
Like everyone he found that every day
That life went on made life more credible
And Saugersville the same as ever before.

'We'd better have a dance,' Earl Backus said.
'There's some that think too much about it all.
They're getting touchy. Yesterday I saw
Bill Countryman as hot as he could be,
And just because Jake Cramer wanted beer
And offered Bill a load of wood for it.
Maybe it wasn't enough, but Bill was mad

And swore that Jake would get no beer from him
And looked as though he meant to knock him down,
And Jake was just as set to do the same.
We'll have a dance and maybe keep our minds
From wondering just how crazy each man is.
Let's say next Saturday night. We'll get Dolf Wick
To find the music and call off the dances.
You put a notice in the store now, Bert.
We'll have a better party than we've seen
Since Grandpa Winterhaus fell down the well.'

The Ladies' Aid served up a splendid feast
With new-killed pork and lots of fried corn mush
Floating in maple syrup, cake and pie
A little coarse, of home-ground flour, but good;
And as the crown, the summit of the feast,
Bert Snyder gave three cans of coffee from
His small and careful store. The odor ran
Along the rooms and hallways of the Grange
And met folk at the door and made them shout.
(The Ladies saved the grounds and took them home
And several households had a washy brew.)
After the lightened tables, cleared and stacked
Against the wall, were gone, Dolf Wick
Stood up and said, 'I know you folks been used
To fancier music than we got here now,
But Rudy Vallee never tried so hard
Nor played with half the will that these boys do.
They aim to please you and I know they will.'

The little man, all grey and shrunk with age,
Was dressed with every care and looked as bright
As a small chickadee whose cheerful voice
Is quite undimmed by snow and winter's storms.
John Backus had a fiddle and his son
Young Richard had a drum; Jake played the horn
And old Ponowski, Ellen Givets' pa,
Wheezed out the tune upon the accordion.
And everybody danced. Not just the young
Or halfway young that usually filled the floor,
But everyone that had a leg to stand
Came out for Lancers and the Virginia Reel.
The girls, who wore their best and looked as gay
Among the older ones as flowers or birds,
Went lightly to and fro. Gert Winterhaus,
The handsomest there — and knew it too — wore red
And tossed her black and curly head and laughed
And found a Grange dance not so bad at all.
May Warder wore a yellow dress that looked
Just like the daffodils in her own yard;
Her eyes were bright as spring, her hair as soft.
She watched John Herbert's back and saw him go
To Gert, and saw them dance, and how they laughed.
But George did not watch Gert. His eyes were on
A slighter figure in the corner where
Amongst the sleepy children Ellen sat.
The most remarkable effect of all
The changes that their world had had to make
Sat there beside her — Givets at a dance!

(29)

Long since had Ellen found how valueless
It was to beg to go, and shut her mouth.
Tonight she nearly fainted when he said,
'Get on your decent dress and get the kids.
We're going down to town tonight to dance.'
His mouth pulled down upon the last two words.
She knew that he had never danced nor would.
Her dress was old and worn upon the seams,
But the warm faded rose brought to her face
What color poverty and work and grief
Had left within her blood. She sat so still,
But smiled at everyone and sang the tune.
When George, who danced with every woman there,
Came and invited her, she looked to Abe
Who said, 'How do George' and said nothing more.
And so she danced, and heard the music swing
Around her head like angel music high,
And weary feet that worked all day were glad
To tread a lighter step, and carried her on.

Roy Smith was like a crazy man that night.
From some small hoard of his or of his friends
He'd swallowed a drink or two, enough to warm
A heart that seemed already warm enough,
Within a body young and powerful.
And if he pined for Gert, no one would know,
Though Gert thought laughing in herself, 'I think
Those eyes are moony when he looks at me.'
She circled twice before she looked again

(30)

To where he stood uproarious at the door
Waving at Adolf Wick across the hall
And making noise enough for seven men —
'Oh land alive he is a handsome man.'

The music lasted till past one o'clock
And everyone was like to drop for tired.
Gus Warder said, 'This is a better dance
Than those we had with fancy orchestras
From Schuylers Falls. There wasn't much to drink,
But all the young men seemed to have good fun
And everyone was gay. Maybe we feel
As though we had our backs against a wall
And must be gay or die. I don't think so.
It looks to me as though we felt so strong
That we could live, and dance, in spite of all.'

The children wondered least of all to find
Their world so changed. To them it was not changed,
For everything at hand was just the same,
And what few times they had been somewheres else
Were soon forgotten in the world of home.
Jack Warder, who was ten, had been to town
Enough to think of stores and bicycles,
And to be sorry for a day or two.
But life was busy in the spring for him.
The fish were jumping down below the dam;
Now it was warmer he could go and build
The house he started in the woods last fall.
He asked his father half a dozen times

Why this had happened and what made it come.
Although he thought that Pa knew everything
He had to be content with 'I don't know.'

Only in school there seemed to be a change,
And that was for the better. Aura Smith,
Who taught the little school and lived at home —
Beyond Ed Winterhaus, the upper road —
Was wholly puzzled by the fearful fate
And asked the Board of Safety what to do.
'There isn't any use in teaching them
About these places which they'll never see,
Because they don't exist, as far as we know.
Maybe they do and we can't see them plain.
Maybe it's in our eyes or in our hearts
And all the world is really just the same.
I've tried to teach them things that would be good
When they were grown, although of course I knew
I taught them lots that they would never use.
But when they learned the population of
The cities of the east, at least I knew
The cities were right there. And you could go
And count the people if you wanted to.
But now — what can I say? What can I teach?'
This was a poser. Five men sat and stared,
And no one made an answer. Backus at last
Spoke slowly with his eyes upon the trees
That showed beyond the window, budded thick.
'There's some things in the past we can't forget,

And kids should know about. So you can teach
The history just the same. And for our life
Even here alone a bit of figuring's good
As ever 'twas. Yes, they should read and write,
Although we haven't much to read and less
To write. Still, all we have should be theirs too,
We cannot give them less than we have had.
About geography, which seems to be
The greatest bother, I should think you'd find
You could cut down, and teach them how things were
And not say how they are, which we don't know.'
Bert Snyder said, 'A different kind of thing
Is what we got to teach these children now.
They've got to learn to make the things they need
Just as folks used to in the days gone by.
We've got a handful still of older ones
Can tell us how to make a candle mould
And fix the fat to fill it, make a spade,
Or hammer out a plow. The girls must learn
To spin and weave, and manufacture soap,
And all the hundred things they'll have to do.'
'I don't see why,' said Countryman, 'they need
Book-learning any more at all. We learned
Because it might be 'twould come handy once
Somewhere outside. But now — there isn't more
Than twenty shelves of books in all the town.
There won't be time for reading either when
The things we got wear out and we must make
All that we need to live by for ourselves.'

Gus Warder spoke, who was a minister's son
And owned at least a quarter of the books
Which Countryman described. 'They have to read
And have to write, they all must learn it well,
Or else before we realize none will know,
And we'll be back to where we started from
More years ago than we can count or tell.
There's too much danger here, as we are now,
That we'll be savages again. I say
They must be taught and made to read although
It wears out every book in town to do.'
Roy nodded, who was fifth and last to speak.
'I guess they ought to read. You can't tell what
May happen yet. It may be good to know.'
Earl Backus waited for a while, then spoke,
'It seems the best that we can do is say
Teach just the same as you've been used to do,
Although geography and such will be
Really a part of history — what we knew
Instead of what we know. Maybe sometime
We can work out a plan, when we can tell
Better than now what children should be taught.
As for the other things Bert speaks about,
We must have school for everyone in those,
And anyone who can remember how
They used to do such things can teach us all.'

V

Unhampered by their grief and loss the spring
Came surely on the brown and soaking land.
Now only in the shadows lay the snow
Which was no longer white but mocked itself
Pretending to be earth all stained with earth.
Upon its melting edges pricks of grass
Greener than hope fulfilled shot up to sun,
And in the woods hepaticas began
To stir within their furry silver hoods.
The clouds came over fast, and moved away,
The rain came down, the sun shone out again.
Old Peter Winterhaus, Ed's uncle Pete,
Ninety-two come fall, said 'Yesterday
I heard the phoebe holler in the woods.'

Across the hills the wind blew sharp and cold
But in the hollows breathed the warmth of spring
And everywhere the water shouted loud.
The creek went roaring like unending surf,
Bank-full and brown and foaming up in cream
In day and night a strong exultant noise.

Ten times a week in all the time he'd lived
In Saugersville John Herbert thought he'd die
Of this slow rural life, the night and day
That moved so slowly on the sloping hills

And brought for him the season s change alone.
He had sickened of the quiet in the nights,
And of the faces which he saw each day
That said the very things they said before —
'Nice day.' 'This wind'll bring some rain tonight,'
'Got winter enough to suit you now, my boy?'
He watched for letters in his little box
Like pigeons bringing news from far away,
And read their message half a dozen times,
Seeing before his eyes the city's life,
Hearing among his trees the traffic roar.
As often as his money would permit,
More often than was good for nerves and heart,
He went to spend a week-end with delight,
Refresh his lungs with gaseous smoky air
And feast his eyes on beauty's ugliness,
Till worn and sick he would come back again,
Cursing his luck and Saugersville as well.
Now since catastrophe he had been stunned,
And waited first to see a world come back
He could not quite believe had gone away.
It did not come. He went to look for it,
Pressed further down the river in his search
Than anyone had gone, but found no more.
    Standing in the shadowy undergrowth,
His eyes upon the river that moved on
So slow, so certain, so mysterious,
He felt his body ache as though his heart
Too worn with journeying had given at last

Acceptance of the ending of his world.
'If I could build a boat' — he turned away,
Shaking his head and kicking at the stones.
He had no skill for such a task, and now
No wish. He could get help perhaps from those
Who knew, and set forth on a voyage to find —
What would he find? He turned back toward the
     hills,
Shifting his rifle in his hand, his eyes
Watching among the trees, his belly gaunt,
And in his heart the fear of nothing known

Some there were that ate the wonder up
And found it lay too heavy on their stomachs,
And brooded nights and said few words all day
Abe Givets, to be sure, was just the same
To all appearance, though none knew the thoughts
That burned the very tissue of his brain —
That he, a free-born citizen, should be
Deprived by such unlikely fate of rights
And privileges that were his very own.
(That others shared them and had lost as well
Was not a part of Givets' grievances.)
But other men were seen to wear thin.
Herbert himself would hardly speak a word,
Although before a pleasant-spoken lad.
But now returning from the river's edge
Bringing no news, his mouth was shut, his eyes
Looked out at nothing from a face of stone.

The greatest change was in old Dick Van Snell,
The wooden-legged man that lived alone
Down in the hollow where the road went dead.
For Dick, though well supplied with poverty,
A cripple and a lonely man, had been
As good a natured man as you could find.
His little shack was set close by the road
On half an ell of land beside the creek,
And there he used to sell some bootleg stuff
And made some cash, enough to keep alive.
He lived alone and yet in company,
For every car that hastened by his door
Brought news to him although it knew it not.
His chair propped back against the shanty wall,
His wooden leg a-cock, his sharp old eyes
Watched makes and number plates, drivers and freight,
And hardly missed a car from morn till night.
The double S that curved on either side
Slowed down the fastest so he saw them well.
'There's Willard with his milk, he's late today;
The kids won't be on time for school again.
That's Harvey Deck, his wife's in with him too.
She must be sick, he wouldn't take her else
To see the doctor or the undertaker.
And Myron Winterhaus, it beats me how
He can find jobs to take him down this way
Past Mary Sawyer's house.' And then the trucks
Whose routing took them past at certain times,
The oil trucks, beer trucks, stone trucks, bread trucks, all

Thundering by his house to shake the walls;
Some dragging trailers, some without, some red,
Some white, some old, some new, but every one
A friend of his, whose driver waved and yelled
'Hey, Dick!' and blew his horn, until the gulf
Echoed again with engine, wheels, and horn.
　　Even at night, when blinding lights flashed in
Upon his poor possessions, on his bed
Which he had set to see the lower curve,
He knew by lights and sound the most that passed
And in his sleep would murmur to himself,
'That's Conway's trucking gang from Oppendam;
There goes the Oklahoma Oil. That's Jack,
And drunk again. What will his woman say?'
　　But now, the road lay still. The grass began
To edge the cracks, the grass so quick to find
The least neglect of man, to push its blades
As sharp as swords and stronger than their steel
Between the firmest stones were ever laid.
The littlest animals had made themselves
At home upon its surface. Insects ran
About their business here and there and built
Their cities in the cracks where now no wind
Ferocious in its sudden passing swirled.
The nights were silent and the water's talk
That had been once a low accompaniment
To intermittent more exciting sounds
Was now a loud monotony of grief
Unbroken as the darkness of the night.

(39)

At dawn old Dick would rise to stare and stare
Both up and down the road and shake his head
And hardly care to eat his scanty meal,
His ears so pressed with silence and his heart
Weighed down with loneliness, his eyes half shut.
And not a word to any when he came
To trade his little stock, now smaller still.
He used to be so full of news and tales
He was the busiest member round the stove
And knew the gossip of the country round.
But now he did not stay, and said no word,
But plodded to the hollow down the road,
His wooden leg a sharp and lonely sound.

Old Grandma Smith was not the least perturbed
By any sense of world default, for she
Ignored steadfastly any sign of change
And clung alone to what had always been.
Rocking her chair with firm, determined tread
She shut her ears to talk of newer ways
That were but older ways come back again —
And she a wise consultant if she would.
Her daughter-in-law Eliza tried to get
Advice on making soap from her who knew
Too well the iron kettle and the smell.
'Go buy your soap,' said Gran and nothing more.
There was a bitter scene when all her store
Of cough-drops — her own favorite kind — was gone,
And Bert had none. In vain Eliza made

A brew of herbs and honey for her throat.
In vain they said, 'We can't go buy you more,'
And told her once again how matters were.
She stormed at them. 'You thankless hearts, you crew
Of faithless children, may Elisha's bears
Come eat you up. I will have none of this
And none of this unlikely lie you tell.
Go leave me be and tell me nothing more.'

The men that did not brood upon their fate
Were driven with restless energy to make
The best of what there was, and plowed and sowed,
And planned and worked to get the most from all.
Gus Warder was a man who used his head
And did his farming there, then on the land.
And now he planned for all and told each one,
As well as he could figure, how much corn
And how much grain and grass and beets and all
They each must have to see the winter through.
The most of them had come and asked him this
And most were glad, but some looked glum and said,
'I guess we know as well as him, we do.'
But Gus and all the Board of Safety men
Were anxious that no weaker links should break
In this close-joined dependent chain which fate
Had forced upon these independent men,
Who had been used to living for themselves
And finding that no easy thing to do.

The summer came upon them like a storm,
A rush of green that swept up over the land
And covered deep the delicate shades of spring
That grew in moister soil and fainter sun.
The grass stood up and stretched in every night.
The new set gardens sprouted thick and green,
And in new fields the grain began to wave.

May Warder in her garden bent her arms
And tugged the hearty weeds from out the rows
Of feathery carrot green. Her garden now
Was flowered with radishes and peas and beans
Instead of blossoms which she loved to grow.
But by the wall the faithful climbing rose
Was breaking into flower and at its foot
Her woodland violets were blooming still.
'I love it, how I love it' in her mind
Went singing on, although she hardly knew
What it could be she loved, unless the smell
Of warming earth and roses newly flowered,
Or sun upon the back, or far the sight
Of birds that circled in a brilliant sky.
She sat back on her heels to look, and then
Felt suddenly a loneliness that bit
And hurt her in her breast until she cried,
And went to work so furious at the weeds
That half the carrots showed their golden sides.

Dolf Wick was nearly eighty and a man
Who weighed each year with speculative thought
And looked both back and forward — though of late
He looked behind more often than before —
Compared the times and valued everything,
And on the whole he thought old times were best.
Now suddenly it seemed to him threescore
Of years that changed so much were changed themselves
And lost away in nothingness till now
The face of things was as it was before
When he was young. Again the trees were tall.
Now here again a larger, stiller breath
Blew in upon a group of families
That walled themselves together against death —
As once before along this creek, he thought,
In days when his great-grandfather was young.
He swelled his chest a bit and said, 'To hell
With all this modern world that came in here
And fixed us with a lot of fancy stuff
We didn't really need. We're just the same
As we were then, just like our ancestors,
And more to start with than they ever had.'
He watched Ed's team come up the village street.
It pleased him now to see the horses go
So constantly upon the concrete road.
He used to say he never learned to like
An engine's sound as well as iron feet.
He waved to Ed and thought within himself,
'We'll show them how to live, those city folks.

We don't need help to keep us safe and warm.'
But then he thought there wasn't anyone,
Most probably, to profit by the show;
And as he turned to go into the house
Again he felt the fierce regret that came
Because his little money which he saved
Had all been put in Continental bonds,
And where were dividends to come from now,
And in what jungle growth of mighty trees
Were capital and interest buried deep?

It happened then as summer came, and work
Was plentiful for more hands than there were,
That even George gave up his lazy ways
And went to work on Abram Givets' farm.
Abe offered him the right to cut his wood
In the back wood-lot, and a bag apiece
Of corn and oats and buckwheat for his food
Come winter, and his keep while working there
Hard under Givets' sharp demanding gaze
George stiffened muscles had been soft for years
And tanned his face and hands and lost some weight.
He wasn't very handy in the fields;
Abe, at half his size, could hoe more rows
And pitch hay twice as quick. But in the barn,
With every animal upon the farm,
George didn't think but knew just what to do.
The three remaining cows of Givets' herd
Would give more milk and easier for George,

The horses came up to the pasture bars
Before he called to them, and even the sows
Suffered his presence near among their young.
    In spite of work and summer sun and Abe,
Whom no one could pretend to like since he
So plainly by his actions said to all,
'I do not like you and expect the same,'
George liked the farm and knew the reason why.
When on the farmhouse stoop the dinner bell
Called from the heated fields to hotter room
The sweating men whose waiting appetite
No heat could quell, George knew that he would find
His reason serving dinner by the stove.
The little Ellen liked to have George there
Because it kept Abe quiet, whose complaints
Had choked her throat a hundred dinnertimes.
He did complain, but not so frequently
And not with blows. Then George's face was new,
A welcome face that was not even unkind
Much less a hostile thing that made you creep.
She came to look for him and felt a pinch
Of disappointment when some farther field
Must needs be worked and Abe would send to him
A child with dinner covered in a pail.
It happened once or twice when Abe was gone
George would appear and ask a drink of milk
And stay and say to her a few slow words
That moved her even while her anxious eyes
Watched the lengthening shadows on the road.

(45)

Abe had no thought of this at all. His mind
Was on more valuable property —
What he could do with money, and his farm.
He thought of rights and privileges denied
By fate and providence, but gave no heed
To robbery of another sort at home.
And Ellen, to be sure, was just as blind
And in her childishness was only glad
That here was someone who was nice to her
And called her pretty-eyes and laughed at her
And stirred a blood which love had never stirred.
George for his part was perfectly intent,
Knew what he wanted, what he meant to get,
And only figured how to get it best
Knowing that Abe was half at least a devil.

VII

Their world's contraction made their blood run
        hot.
Not only that the young men looked at home
For every chance of love, but felt besides
A fierce desire to carry on this home,
Asserting by their potency their power
To outface fate and make mankind survive.
And other men with wives were eager too
And found new life in effort and in fear,
Seeing themselves alone among these hills

And, shuddering at the wilderness without,
Desired more lovingly their homes and wives;
And more than one smiled to herself; but some
Remembered doctors too were gone, and feared.

With disappointment harsh upon his tongue
John Herbert felt at last he must give up
The world he knew and what it meant to him,
Accept the steep horizon which now bound
Himself and twice a hundred more in one.
And seek for any solace he could find.
'For what is Saugersville to me,' he said,
'Only a desert island where I live
Because I can live nowhere else but here.
Death in the city would have been to me
No more than death, but here I live and die
And have no being worth the name of life.
I am no part of this community;
Their ideas are not mine. I will not live
A narrow choked and miserable life
Save as I must, which will be bad enough.'
He went to get his gun, to hunt his food,
And seeing it was moved to say again,
'I will not live a miserable life.
I do not have to live my life at all,
And know the key to silence if I need.'

The only other one in Saugersville
Who cared about the outside world so much

That loss without seemed more than need within
Was Gertrude Winterhaus, who looked to find
Like John some compensation for her loss.
It did not take them long to find in each
A ready ear, and equally sad complaint.
They talked of city lights and shows and songs,
Nostalgic as two pole discoverers
Huddled in an igloo in the snow.
He did not like her really, for her wit
Was on the surface like her handsome ways.
She might be quick and eager as a bird
With plumage shining like the lovely jay's,
But like the lovely jay her voice was harsh,
Her laugh too sudden and her eye too bold.
Of far and secret inner depths that flowed
Not dark but hidden in his inmost mind
She saw no trace and cared no whit at all.
But for the time indeed he was content
To play upon the surface when the depths
Offered such opportunity for pain.

    The summer gave them sweet and shining nights
And many lovely places in the green
Recesses which she knew, and not alone
From childhood exploration but of late,
She who was the belle of Saugersville.
Returning late at night to his own house
He thought, 'I do not want to marry her;
I do not love her nor does she love me,
And yet before we know we'll be engaged.'

Maria worried over Gertrude's ways
And wept to find her acting as she feared
She always acted when away from home.
Her feeble countermands made Gertrude laugh,
And easy-going Ed would never frown.
'She's young and wants her fun; you let her be.'
Her so-called virtue Gert was quick to guard,
Knowing the fierceness of the little round
Of gossip and the strict communal ways,
And knowing well its value if she lived
Forever here where everyone knew all.

Young Robert Munn, who kept the one garage,
Had lost his job most certainly of all.
His gasoline had been divided up
But for a hundred gallons in reserve.
And some had used their farm machinery
Until their share was gone; others had kept
Theirs put away or used it miserly.
There was some work on various machines,
But few were now employed and he was left
To tend his garden and to chop his wood
And figure how to use his hard-earned skill
Which once had served him well and made him rich
By village standards. Robert kept his house
Well painted, with a furnace in the cellar,
His pretty wife in pretty clothes, two cars,
One for his business and a pleasure car,
And felt he was the coming man in town.

But now he **was a** poorer man than most,
With little strength to work upon the land
And little knowledge of the farming job;
But work he must and did to live at all.
   He and his Bessie were deprived of more
Because more cash had brought them from the **store**
More boughten goods, to eat, to wear, to use.
And Robert, who when things went well was **gay**
And somber when they didn't, as are all,
But he more gay more somber, felt the depths
Of fierce despair that wakened him at night
For all the achings of his weary frame.
Not he nor anyone in Saugersville
Could feel a wholly personal despair
Since equally on all the burden fell;
But Robert, whose well-earned prosperity
Had faded with the world from which it grew,
Was tortured by an individual grief
That he must bow his head who had been **proud**.
Young Bessie was so loving and so close
That she must feel it too, although she cared
Mainly because of him; until the day
When rising early to prepare his food
That he might meet the sun at work, she felt
The waves of nausea that pushed her down
And knew that what she thought and feared **was**
      true.
She said no word to Robert, for she knew
How hard upon his head this news would break.

Till he, who even in despondency
Was always loving, full of care for her,
Noticed, and saw, and understood, and wept.

His ordinary life for Reverend Yule
Was not so different now; his shed was full
Of well-split wood, his chickens still laid eggs,
And he was given flour and milk, and made
From his tall maple trees his sugar brown.
Though there were some who said, in muttered breath,
The old man and his wife were useless weight,
The most were glad to take their pay in words,
Not only Sundays when the lightnings flashed,
But weekdays in a gentler kind of talk.
No man more eager than this parson now
To be of aid, to offer what he could.
He battled down his shyness, his desire
To sink into himself, his shadowy thoughts
And speculations on another life,
In order to come out and fight in this.
There were not many who asked help of him
By speaking out directly; but they came
To ease their minds of overwhelming awe
And fear and wonder and a kind of pain
Of newness at the different state of things.
To minds worn down by years of changelessness
The sudden earthquake of familiar ways
Brought agony of thinking and despair.
There were not many who were sure of God

And sure this was his will; they did not ask
The minister concerning this, but talked
Of crops and cattle and the old new arts
Which now they learned from elders such as he.
The still courageous face, the quiet eyes
That knew the wakening of an inner fire
That burned and sank but did not ever die —
These counselled them of strength and will to toil
And sent them home refreshed and comforted.
    They did not know the dark uncertain nights
When Ephraim Yule demanded of his God
The reason for the destruction of his world,
And listening heard no answer, and despaired,
Until the deepest hours when all the stars
Are moving out of sight behind the sky
And what there is of outer strength for man
Must rally to him then, for he has none —
The minister found it, whether God or no,
And faced his people with a quiet heart.

VIII

It seemed as though the summer had not been
So quick was it departed, and the nights
Tasting of chill, the days of apple smell.
May Warder covered her tomato vines
With rhubarb leaves against the chance of frost.
Beside the mill Jake Cramer cleaned his trees

Of every apple — seven barrels full.
And chimneys smoked with all the busy stoves
Where women canned and bottled everything
That could be saved and kept for winter's use.
Upon the hill John Herbert dug a hole
For winter vegetables, and saw the red
Come on the maple tree beside the road.
Gus watched the corn as dearly as a mother
And prayed the frost would keep until next moon.
  His wife was thinking of another kind
Of frost that comes before its time, and said,
'Gus, May's not looking good, I don't know why.'
She had suspicions but she let them lie,
And thought he might say something to agree.
'Well, I don't know. Maybe she works too hard.
She's always quiet and no quieter now.'
'Oh, men,' sighed Mabel to herself, and then,
'It makes a body worry so these days,
The way we are, no doctor or no nurse.
You can't help fearing somebody'll fall sick.'
'Oh let that be,' said Gus. 'She's not sick yet,
Nor like to be, a healthy girl like her.
I know she's pale, but make her drink more milk,
And if you need to, get Maria in
To help you out, and let May rest a bit.'
His wife said nothing, but resolved to have
A talk with May, although she knew too well
For all the love between them, she would fail,
And find no answer for her worried heart.

The summer had made clear to May the truth
That he cared nothing for her. Every day
Or so it seemed, she saw the two of them
Together, heard them speak of one another,
And saw within her mind a close embrace.
At picnics in the summer, when they went
In those cool woods above the waterfall
Where limestone rocks had made a sort of cave,
'Twas always John and Gert that went alone
To explore its chambers with a candle end,
Or hide in spray behind the outsprung fall.
And hence together were the other two,
May and Roy Smith, and good friends to be sure,
But each the lover of another heart,
Impatient, miserable, and hard to please.
They did not speak of what they both well knew,
And made no accusations nor complaint,
But clung together when those other two
Went brazenly apart and looked not back.

Now John was weary in his mind of Gert,
But mind was not the captain to command,
And he could feel he would capitulate
To orders he would rather not have given.
His house was lonelier than ever now,
His nights more wakeful and his tender nerves,
Too near the surface at the quietest times,
Were like a festering wound that will not heal.
Though many a night before this later fate

Had found him brooding on unkindly life,
Now he would weep, or shiver with the cold,
And find no solace anywhere at all.
Distrustful of a creed, he did not go
To talk with Reverend Yule, though if he had
He might have found a clearer mind than his
To show if not the why the how of life.
He talked with no one really, only Gert,
And that was only reminiscences
Of what there might have been, not what there was.
Seeing no better wall for loneliness
And desperate nights, he thought at last he must
Propound the question which he knew would have
An answer which he did not want to hear.

Days got a chill which made Bert light his stove
And brought together once again the House
That sat and steamed and talked and hacked and spit
And settled what to do and how and when —
Provided that the Board confirmed it too.
But when the grey beards wagged about the stove
The talk was all of fifty years ago,
The what had been, the past that had come back
To throw its shadow on these present days.
'When we were young,' said Dolf, 'in olden days,
We didn't think to look to anywheres
But here to have our fun. Of course the fairs
Were in the towns, but only once a year.
The rest of the time there were so many bees,

All kinds of bees, when folks would husk their corn,
Or raise a house; most any excuse would do
To get the folks together, work and play.
Then there was general training when the men
Would meet and train, and all the women too
Would come to watch the men-folks strut themselves.
Then in winter we'd go visiting round —
There wa'n't no work to do — to see our friends —
Leave in the morning when the chores were done,
And spend the day, and eat all you could hold —
That being the women's pride, to set more food
Than anyone could eat; my, it was good;
There ain't no pride in cooking nowadays —
And then drive home to feed and milk the cows,
The sleighbells ringing in the dark and snow.
And then folks took to driving cars and went
So far, and saw so many things, so new,
They weren't content to play at home no more.
I guess the movies got to be for them
What fairs and bees and dances used to be,
If they could see some fancy show like that
They didn't need to visit with their friends.
And now you see it's like it used to be.
We've got no movies nor no cars to drive;
We must stick home, and do the best we can.
I think it's better now as it used to be.'
John Backus filled his pipe and lit a match,
But halfway to the bowl he stopped to speak.
'There's something else to that I tell you, Dolf,

That's part of it. Now I remember well
When Saugersville set fashions for itself,
I mean to say we had our own ways here
That weren't the ways of Centerfield or Steck,
Much less the ways of any city place
Where most of us had never been at all.
What ways were good and what were not we knew
And needed no one else to tell us which.
And no one wanted to be richer then
Than old Dave Vanderbeck, that lived right here
And had a carpet on his bedroom floor.'
The match burnt out; he lit another one
And puffed his pipe, and took it out and said,
'We wanted houses that were neat and clean,
Tight in the winter, good, and solid built,
With furniture to use, and please the eye.
We wanted plenty in the cellar room
To pile the table heavy all the year,
And cider in the barrel getting hard.
A nice-matched team of horses was the most
A man could want besides his house and farm.'
He shook his head and spit into the box.
'And then — you know the way it went; the wife
Would travel over to Schuylers Falls and see
Some brand newfangled stove her cousin had,
And work to get one like it till she did.
Or else the movies made her think her clothes
Were just not fit to wear, although that coat
Had got at least three years' more wear in it.

Don't blame it all upon the women-folks.
We're just as bad, with cars and radios.
And every cent we spent on them two things
Would cost us twenty cents before we're through,
Because they showed us things we had to buy
Or thought we had, which costs about the same. —
Oh well they're gone, and money too is gone.
We didn't want this, but we're free again
To follow out the ways we think are best,
And try our hands again at right and wrong,
And set the fashions now for Saugersville.'

II

☆

I

OCTOBER first now brought them half a year
Completed in this world that was so new
And so tarnation old. They were the same,
Men and boys and girls and wives and maids,
As on that midnight in the spring of fate,
The same as on the day before that night
That saw the last strange wheels go down their
       road.
But in each heart burned now a stronger fire
That flamed because of darkness roundabout
And burned the brighter for the winds that blew.
United by the implacable forest wall
That hung behind the cultivated hills,
United more by fear and need of strength,
They knew each other as they never had,
And bonds that irked were still dependable.
The horror of catastrophe had gone
As even horror must, into past time.
The sense of doom was there, but buried deep
In hearts that mostly only longed to live
And looked to find the means through all the days.
Their eyes looked now to winter and the snow,
The test to search them out, if they were strong.
They knew the answer if their strength should fail.

But one there was whom thought of winter shook
More coldly than the rest, who moaned at night
And turned and turned and waited for the light,
And watching sunrise wished for night again,
Thinking of snow and bitter days alone;
Though all his days were lonely, it was worse
To know you could not travel if you wished.
So Dick Van Snell met fall with shaking lips,
And if he slept woke always with a cry
Hearing again upon the road his wheels.
Seeing the man come slowly to the store,
Bringing the jug of cider which he used
To trade for food — hard cider too,
As good as any washed a gullet yet;
And Dick had found his ample store more good
Than if his barrelsfull went down his throat;
(This jug the next to last, and then what then?) —
Seeing him come so slowly, and his face
All loose with loneliness and grief, Earl said,
'Now Dick, here's something I've been thinking of.
The winter's coming, and I need a man
To help split wood and other chores about.
Come cold, why don't you come and live with us?
I'll feed and lodge you for the work you do.'
He knew Earl meant it kindly, but he said,
'I guess I'll stick down by my place awhile.'
'It's lonely there, and most a mile beyond
The Havins' place; you'd better come up here.
There's room enough, and food, and company.'

'No, no. I'll stay at home. I like it there.'
He took his little load and headed home,
Thinking with fierce distaste of any house
Where he might live except his own, his own.
The Backus farm was set back on the hill;
You could not see the road, a little road
That even in other days had few to pass,
The trees were all around it like a wall.
If he must live, and life was hardly worth
The trouble that it took to eat, to breathe,
He would be here upon the road, his road,
And if by some unapprehended chance
This bitter state of things should cease to be,
There he would wait to hear the wheels again,
To watch the world come rolling by his door.
  His house was dark, he lit a candle end,
Threw wood upon the fire, and ate some meat
Left over from his hunt of yesterday.
The silence burned his ears. He looked about
And counted all he saw his own, and yet —
Now to what end should he stay here, alone?
And wall himself within his house, alone?
And there await a world now gone, alone?
The jug of cider on the corner shelf
Seemed to provide an answer, or at least
Some solace if no answer could be found.
Regardless of its worth and rarity
He drew the plug and set to work to drink.

Seeking the last of summer and its sun
That was not now so burning bright as trees
Turned riotous and ruddy with the cold,
John Herbert and his Gertrude went to walk,
He with his gun against the chance of meat,
She with a line and hook for other food.
Below the Havins' place, before the gulf
Enclosed in shadow both the brook and road
The Sauger's widened to a quiet pool
Hung over by a rock, a fishes' haven —
And Gertrude was the one to catch them out.
But John was restless and his feet were loud
In leaves upon the bank. She scolded him
And he grew sultry, for his heart was tried
And bitter with his unresolved desire.
At last they quarrelled and the words were hot
And glittered in the pale descending sun
And hurt them both and festered in the blood.
Until in rage he took her by the arms
And shook her hard, and she came close and fought.
So then at last they clasped each other tight
And anger seemed to do what love could not,
Hot as they were and burnt beyond control.
A part of him that was not so stood out
And watched and hated him and said, you fool,
The while his hands were busy at her breast.
And she as well could not be wholly mad
But said deep in her mind, 'I've got him now.
We'll have to marry if we like or not.'

He pulled her down upon the ground. The leaves
Of willows dropped about them and the creek
Made unregenerate noises in its bed.
    The road was fifty yards away, as still
As that old Indian trail that used to run
Among the ancient hemlocks on the bank.
Even the wind was still. And then a sound,
A shattering shot broke out, and slammed their ears
And wrenched their minds and made them both jump
        up,
Leaving with some regret and some relief
Their purpose and desire behind them with
The impress of their bodies in the grass.
'Who would be hunting here?' said John aloud,
'So near to Dick Van Snell's — his house is there
Beyond the curve. We'd better go and see.'
They reached the road but had not far to go
To see upon its surface what replied
To all their questions and its own as well.
For here upon the cracking grass-grown road
And at the curve where trucks were used to blow
Their horns to warn him of their passing by,
And where the lights at night struck on his house,
Here where no one could stand in other days
For fear of sudden death around the curve,
Here Dick Van Snell had ended his own life,
Seeing no reason not to leave a world
Which had already left him, taking away
All that he cared for, all his life for him.

Earl Backus thought, 'I should have made him come.
This is my fault, or partly. Well, I tried.
He had not much to live for, true enough.'
He stood a moment by the empty grave
That would be filled so soon. It was the first
In Saugersville since fate had marked them out.
The ground was not yet frozen and the smell
Of earth rose up and smote him like a blow.
He sighed and looked to where the hills
Rolled back in ridges to the distant sky,
First showing in their colors, then afar
One blank and uncommunicative blue.
He said aloud, 'Now Dick, 'twas easy done —
You had no chick nor child to think upon,
Nor any cared if you were quick or dead —
Not many men are free to do their will.'
He thought of Mate, his wife, their crippled girl,
And even of the town, that looked to him
For guiding where there were few hands to guide.
The weariness of living and despair,
The fear of doom that waited in his heart
And knew no date for fear to fasten on,
The weight of strength this small embattled group
Required of him and found in him each day —
These bore him down, and for this moment here
He thought of Dick and thought he had done well.
   The wild geese cried above him in the sun,
The geese that flew as certain of their goal
As though no world of men had been wiped out —

(64)

No doubt they thought it for their good alone
That lakes were free and men and guns were few —
And with that stirring cry Earl turned again
And saw below the hillside plot of graves
The village visible through thinning leaves,
A compact shining group of white and grey
Below the V of birds that passed so high.
A fierce convulsion tightened up his chest,
He clenched his hands and dug his heels in earth.
'This is our place, by life and death and work;
We've lost one man, we must be strong to live
And fight this enemy we cannot see
Our weakness and our loneliness and fear;
We must be strong or we will all lie here.'

II

Abe Givets thought, 'He was a puny man
To give up rights and privileges
And hang ahold of just that one — the right,
Or so some say it is — the right to die.
In spite of all we've been deprived of here —
And by what law 'twas done I'd like to know —
I'll say for one I'm not the man to die,
But mean to live and get the best of things.'
Now what he meant by 'get the best of things'
Was hatching in a plan within his brain
That looked always to the main — or Givets' — chance.

Off to the westward of his house the fields
Sloped sharply down and met a fringe of trees.
Below that bank a small wild hollow lay,
A tangled place and waterless; and there
Amongst the rocks that showed on every side
A great hole gaped, deep in the ground, —
A curious ugly place, cut down in rock
By some old underground collapse that sent
The surface down into the earth and left
This dangerous and mysterious aperture.
There shone the bones of many hapless cows,
That, strayed or thrown in dead, had left
Chalky mementos in the damp and gloom.
Curious children every year or so
Would view the place and throw some rocks below.
And once Roy Smith, before he was half grown,
Had rigged a rope and let himself down in,
A candle in his pocket. He could see
From where his feet struck bottom nothing much
But walls of rock and all the dark debris
Of years about him on the rocky floor.
Even his heart the damp had chilled, and sent
Him climbing out to daylight and the sun.
    Now Abe had need of stone to make a wall,
His fences broken and no wire to hand,
And brought his team, with George along to help,
Down in the field beside the fringe of trees
As near the hole as they could get.
And he and George picked likely stones and rolled

Or carried them together to the cart.
They worked about the mouth, a tricky job,
For stones were loose and slid and clattered down;
A man might fall as well with softer sound,
But here the best and handiest stones were found.
They had almost a load and needed one
To top it off, which Abe went back to get
While George turned round the team. There at the edge
Abe looked down in, the first he had today,
And saw that frost or rain or age had sunk
One part of the great hole, down at one side
Far, far below. There water glistened now
Where had been only damp and chill before.
He saw it shine; and something else as well,
A glimmer of whiteness at the water's edge
Like frost or snow. But now the air was warm
And even down there it could not be that cold.
He stared and stared and drew his shoulders in
And wrapped his arms about himself and stared.
Then hearing George, that reined the horses in,
He went back quickly from the hole and said,
'Now George we've got enough. That was too big
And fastened down too hard. We'll let it go.
We won't have time to draw more stone today.'
George thought, 'I never knew Abe leave behind
A thing he set to get. He must be tired,
But tired is something that he never is.'

 At home that night, with Ellen gone to bed,
Abe sat beside the table thinking hard

Of that small gleaming whiteness in the hole.
'There used to be a tale, I mind it well,
My old granduncle telling me, that once
The Indians came to get their salt above
Our farm, back in the hollow by his place —
A spring that disappeared so long ago
Not even his grandfather ever saw it.
Maybe it went down underground and now
Has burst out in my hole. Maybe there was
Always some salt down there, but no one went
To get it out of such a dangerous place.'
He laughed low to himself, an ugly sound
That fluttered the candle and awoke the dog.

Next day he made a ladder in the barn
Of rope and slats, and nailed it to a tree
Above his hole, and made his way below —
A dangerous journey, but he feared it not.
His dream was true. The crystals tasted salt.
The water too. It could be boiled to leave
The precious grains that would make Givets rich.
He scraped away the white so nothing showed,
And climbed his ropes, and hid them in the tree,
Then silent as a buzzard in the sky
Awaited time that was to be his own.

George did not think of anything these days
Except the woman that he wanted most.
He did not contemplate his other days
With brighter birds of love than this small wren,

And certainly he had forgot his wife.
He only knew he wanted Ellen most,
And thought by now she wanted him as well.
   The summer's ending waked in Ellen's heart
A kind of restlessness she had not known
Since windy days in childhood on the hill
Where all the countryside lay spread to see
And she, wind-blown, a small and eager thing,
Had longed to go, to see, to find, to live.
Now George's hand that sometimes handled hers
Could bring the same vibration to the blood,
The same deep breath, the sense of warm desire.
She waited for him now, and watched him come,
And saddened when he went. Her eyes were bright,
Her cheeks had even color and her hair
Shone with more brushing than it ever had.
Even the husband that denied her life
Could not prevent the quickening of her breath.
She thought less now of Abe's dark cruel ways,
And fear, which made her clumsy, lessened too.
She went about the little ugly house
With grace and eagerness, as though a light
Were shining in her always even there.

III

May Warder fought the summer's battles through
And kept her heart in bounds, that would leap out,

Seeing the man she loved and her he loved
Go always hand in hand forgetting her.
By fall she thought, 'I am recovering now;
This sickness is not fatal; I will live,
And likely love some man that will love me.'
But nothing that she felt supported this.
The death of Dick Van Snell meant only that
Again she knew these two were out alone.
She did not know this time would be the last.
She put him from her mind as best she could,
And watched the other single men and boys,
Knowing that she would marry one of them,
Or never marry, in their island world.

Today she went to Bessie Munn's, to help
With work that Bessie was hard put to do,
Now growing large and always miserable.
She went there every week to help and cheer;
She wanted no return, but Robert tried
To help her father any way he could.
May did the wash, as Bessie sat and sewed,
Making from scraps of cloth she had put by
The clothes she needed for the waiting one.
They talked of all the news in Saugersville.
Which having but itself to talk of found
In every least detail something to tell.
'They say that Mr. Yule looks poorly now.
I haven't seen him much, not going to church.'
'I hear Ed's horse he liked so much is dead,

The red, white-footed one he's had for years.'
'And every horse we got is needed bad,
There are some colts, but they're no good to work.
There'll be a time when most we have are gone
Before the ones we raise are old enough.'
May, like her father, looked ahead and planned,
But planning was a chancy thing in days
When this today might be the end of all.
She saw the tears come into Bessie's eyes
That mostly nowadays were filled with tears,
And shook herself and wrung out all the clothes.
'We're doing pretty well, we pioneers,
Surely as well as our great-grandmas did,
Although it's harder for us, knowing how
To live another and an easier way.
I guess it's like all pioneering too.
The women get the worst, but they're the best
And bravest always. You know that now, Bess.'
So Bessie dried her tears and tried to think
Of how her great-great-grandmother had come
To settle in these parts before the war,
And spent the winter in a covered sleigh
Before their hut was built, and bore her child
By its rude hearth, their first established home.
      The clothes hung out, May said good-bye and went
Downstreet to see if Bert could let her have
A spool of thread she needed for a dress.
The store was empty, as it often was,
No more the going in and coming out,

The heavy feet upon the deep-worn sill,
The old latch clicking with the earthy hands.
The stove was lit, the men still came and sat
About its warmth, the council of the old,
That could not leave their habits if they tried.
But now there was no changing to and fro,
No trucks that stopped to bring the store more goods,
No mail man, waited by the daily crowd.
Bert stayed there always — habit there again,
Though few there were to buy and few to sell —
A little trade in things some people had
And others did not have — butter or eggs,
Honey and syrup, apples, pears, or quince;
But of the goods, the irreplaceable goods,
Division had been made and record taken.
Bert counted up his spools and searched the list.
'Your mother had one black, one white, last month,
You've right to half a dozen more, I see,
Three white, three colored. Take your choice here, May.
The pretty spools were like a row of flowers.
She picked the yellow that she liked so well,
And saw him write her name, 'One spool of thread,'
And thought of that old store-book Father had
Where every old inhabitant was named
And what they bought, and when, how much it cost
In pounds and pence, so old a book it was,
So that you saw them in the vanished store
Buy Hyson tea and indigo and nails
And every other one a gill of rum.

Thinking of them and what she said to Bess,
She filled her lungs with air that seemed to give
A strength like theirs to all who still lived here
And followed in their ways and fought their fight.

Not since that day more sultry in their hearts
Than in the autumn sunshine by the pool
Had John and Gertrude met; as though that day,
That spanned both life and death so close, so strong,
That brought their bodies to the burning edge
And froze them stiff with horror at the sight
Of death so weary and intolerant,
Had showed them both a knowledge that was old
Within their hearts but only now made clear,
That said to each, 'Look, this is not the one.'
So that they shunned each other, shamed enough
That such relief should gather in their hearts.
    For once Maria found her girl some help.
Gert did her chores with no complaints, and stayed
At home until her father said, 'Now Gert,
Your feller ain't been round this way at all.
What's come to him? Maybe he's gone away
Down river like he did that other time.
I guess he won't be finding more'n he did,
And might as well make up his mind to stay.'
'If you mean John,' said Gert, who knew quite well
All that he meant and more than what he said,
'He's not my feller nor intends to be,
Nor I intend to have him.' Maria looked

(73)

Behind Gert's back at Ed and shook her head,
So he said nothing but went back to read
The Bible, which he read of evenings now,
Which did not serve as well as papers did
For sleeping under; but he found it good
And read laboriously the Book of Job.

Ede Salzenbach knew more than anyone
About all business which was not her own
And was not prone to keep it to herself.
Her house was right across the street from Bert's,
Her kitchen on the side where she could see
Each car and team that stopped, and stood, and went;
They said she knew how many hairs there were
In every horse's tail that went that way.
Whatever facts she had she did not wait
To find them true before repeating them,
Or if she lacked, conjecture gave the rest.
And now she said that Gert had jilted John,
  After the way they carried on,' she said.
'I'd think it shame to act the way they did
And not get married afterwards for keeps.'

Embittered by the knowledge that his life
Was no more private than all other lives
That lived so close, so open to the gaze,
John suffered half from disappointed love —
Desire perhaps would be the better word —
And half from publicly reviewed chagrin

That he must play the part of failure here,
When really he was glad, and wished to say so.
   Before at least there had been Gert for talk,
But now his words grew bottled up within
Until at last in need he tried the man
Whose work he scorned and thought of no account
Beyond the store an open space of land,
A sort of common, gave a pleasant air
To those few houses, set on either side,
Their backs against the hills, that were the best,
The neatest, most substantial in the town —
Ede Salzenbach's, the Cramers', and the Yules',
With one or two between not quite so proud.
The minister's house faced out on all the rest
Across the common's end, as though it watched
With quiet shining eyes the secular world,
Not so much in reproof as kindliness, —
Its yellow clapboards faded in the sun
Its aged roof a soft, declining grey.
Descending from his hillside to the town
In late November light that shone and paled
And left the valley deepening into night,
John Herbert thought, 'This is a quiet place' —
The first time he had thought like that in praise,
He who despaired in its monotony.
So coming to the doorway in the dusk
He felt already in his heart some hope
That life was better than he thought it was,
And even if it wasn't, men might bear

(75)

Troubles like his with equanimity.
　　The minister was cracking butternuts
From last year's crop, well dried and wrinkled black,
The very devil to crack, but paying well
With sweet, rich meats the hammer and the toil.
Seeing who came, the reverend pushed away
Hammer and iron and bowl of nuts, and gave
His guest a handful of his hard-won prize.
The two had never met to talk like this;
At first they tried each other out to see
What thoughts there were behind the wall of words,
What title each could give to reason's name.
At last John said, 'Do you know what to think
Of this our special fate, these seven months
Of isolation in a world destroyed?
Don't tell me God, or Providence, has willed
That this be so, not any other so.
What do you really think the answer is?'
The old man moved his hands and turned them up.
His candle shone on weathered, empty palms.
'You know there is no answer to this thing
Except the one that means two things to us —
The one you will not have, and I can give
No other to your question, as you know
And if I say God in his wisdom made
The mystery; and if you say blind fate
Playing an aimless game let fall this trick,
Why, what's the difference? We're bound to live
Because some strength within us says we must;

It's taking all our time to find out how
And keep the breath within us warm.' He paused
And watched John's face and said again, 'I see
You think there is a difference. I too —
I have not always felt as I do now
Submission to God's will in this his world,
Nor can I counsel that you bow your head,
For youth must fight and with its fighting learn.'
The younger man said then, 'I've fought so long
And learned so little that I'm tired of it.
My life was never much of a success,
Although it looked to be before I found
That I must leave it all to go away
And spend my days in quiet in the air.
But here again I have not made my life
What I would have it be. I used to think
Forever of the city, all it meant,
And thought I could do nothing if not there.
And when I found not being there had saved
The life I valued nowhere else, why then
What had I left? I have been lost, and done
More than one foolish thing in loneliness.'
The old man smiled and looked at him and said,
'But now those things are past?' And John said, 'Yes';
And that was all the requiem for Gert.

When John went home, and it was late that night,
He felt his heart beat lighter in his breast
And watched the stars come up behind the hill

(77)

And thought they looked more kindly on his house
That showed a gable-end against the sky
Than they had used to look in nights gone by.

IV

November days were very cold and still
With yet no snow to cover frozen fields;
The roads were rock, whereon the horses' hoofs
Sounded like blows, their breaths were thick as smoke,
And every teamster jumped and clapped his arms.
Earl Backus, piling his potatoes up
In bins waist-high against the cellar wall —
A hearty bunch of sober-sided spuds —
Attempted once again to figure up
The tale of villagers, their heads and needs,
And what they had to fight the winter with.
'I know there's some we'll have to help to live
Before the snow is gone; there's bound to be,
And none of us will be right smart by spring.
But spring we'll see, and all of us, I hope,
Providing what has come don't come to us.'
He shook his head and shut the cover down
And went upstairs, whistling a tune to hide
The thought that maybe one, his crippled girl,
Would not be here to see the snowdrifts go.

On Saturday nights the men still went to Bill's,
Although he had no beer to offer them,

And cider was still sweet inside the keg.
Bill leant across the bar and said, 'Next year
I'm going to grow some hops. I found a place
Where they grow wild, what's left I guess
Of someone's hop yard twenty years ago.
You'll see some beer will make you smack your lips.'
He grinned, his easy face red in the light
Of half a dozen candles on the bar.
Around the table four attentive heads
Bent over pinochle cards. Some others watched,
And others tipped their chairs back on the wall
Behind the stove, and talked and coughed and spat.
Sometimes they grouched about nothing to drink.
'Our old stone mill down on the holler road
Was built for a distillery, they say,
Way back before the Civil War,' said Bill.
'But no one now knows how to make the stuff.
You have to have more tools than we have got.'
'Yes, I remember it,' said Adolf Wick.
'When I was a boy they still made whiskey there.
The difference between folks then and now,
They didn't have as much as we have here,
But made the most of what they had, while we
Can hardly handle what we've got to hand
Much less go figure out some new ideas.'
'There may be time for that,' John Backus said.
'We've only just begun to live these lives
Since we were born in this new world last spring.
You can't expect such babies to be smart.

(79)

Give us some time, we'll make as many things
And have as many comforts as they had.'
They all began to talk at once, each man
With some idea he had been pondering on
To fill a need now newly felt again;
As though their minds, long dulled with great supply
Of every tool to hand, had come alive,
And that thin streak of sharp inventiveness
That Yankee minds have never wholly lost
Sprang into action and went hard to work.
'I'm goin' to hitch my thrasher to a horse.' —
'I'm going to build a little water wheel.' —
'I think that I can fix that engine up,
That old steam engine that my uncle had.
It used to go real well. You could burn wood.' —
'Young Robert Munn says maybe he can make
A dynamo and harness up the creek
And make some electricity of our own.'
That was the best idea; they turned to Jake
The miller: 'Couldn't we use that wheel of yours?' —
They talked on late that night and quite forgot
How sober they had been with naught to drink,
Intoxicated by their own designs.
    'It's very well to talk about such things,'
Said Mrs. Cramer as they went to bed
And Jake was telling her about the plans.
'But there's some things we really got to have,
And that before next summer or next spring,
And one of them is salt. The last bag's gone

Out of the mill. It's all divided up,
And though I s'pose some folks have got some still,
The cattle need it now. They'll need it bad
'Fore many weeks, and folks will need it too.'
Jake did not relish much the thought of food
Without its savor; and knew no answer either
To where it could be found; so went to sleep
And dreamt of pickling hams in maple sugar.

Thanksgiving came and went and still no snow
They kept no great festivity that day,
Though Reverend Yule reminded them indeed
How fortunate they were to be alive
And well provided for, their cellars full,
Their barns stuffed out to bursting and the shocks
Of hay and corn still standing in the fields —
'More blessed far than those impoverished ones
Who faced the winter in Massachusetts Bay
With little food and no conveniences
Their backs against the wilderness of death.
And though we are more lonely even than they
And face a peril that is yet unknown,
We have their courage and three hundred years
Of courage on American frontiers
To make us brave and steadfast even here,
Even upon the last of all frontiers.'
   But in their homes some shook their heads and sighed
And thought how many men had starved to death
To make the nation which was now no more.

While others sat around a festal board
No less well burdened than it ever was.
Maria Winterhaus was proud of hers.
The turkey, which she raised, was big and fat,
The pork was newly killed, a noble pig
With noble spare-ribs, browned just to a turn.
Pickles and sauce and even cranberries
From the cedar swamp, put up last summertime,
A little sour for lack of sugar to spare,
But excellent, and she was proud of them.
The pumpkin pie was just as good as ever.
The family did full justice to the food.
The Countrymans were there — Bill's wife and Ed
Were brother and sister; and Bill's mother too,
Who had no teeth but managed to consume
At least as much as anybody else.
They talked of other Thanksgivings, of days
When all the families came home to dine
And there would be a score at any table.
'Folks had good families in those days,' said Ed,
'Half a dozen children anyway, and more.'
'They needed 'em,' said old Mis' Countryman,
'And need 'em now again. You young folks here
Had better get to work.' She leered at Gert,
And made the younger boy, Eugene, turn red.
  'Those days of going places don't seem real.'
Bill pulled his waistcoat down, shook off the crumbs
'We used to be a-travelling all the time,
But I don't miss it much. It don't seem real,

As though we ain't the same as we were then.'
'Maria's cooking's just the same,' said Lize.
'I don't see how you do it nowadays.'
Maria laughed, pretending not to care.
'I guess it ain't so good. We get along
And have most things the same. But I declare
I don't know what we'll do without no salt.'
'We'll have to get it someways pretty soon.
I'm damned if I know how,' said Countryman.
Young Ed, the older boy, spoke up: 'Roy Smith
Allows that he could go and find some salt
Out west of here, where Swago used to be.
The salt would still be there, he says.' The boy
Was shining at the thought of such a trip.
'It's more'n a hundred miles to there,' said Ed,
'And hard to find the way, with all roads gone.'
'And God knows what to meet him on the way. —
The women shook their heads, the men thought how
This could be done, to go and then bring back
Sufficient salt for all, if salt there was.
To Gert, who had said nothing all this time,
Not liking family feasts or family talk,
There came a sudden and surprising pull
Somewhere beneath her heart. With more distaste
Than any other feeling she reviewed
Her thoughts and found uprising there in her
A sudden fear and sorrow and regret
That Roy — whom she disliked — should go so far
And face upon so bold an escapade

(83)

All dangers of a known and common kind
As cold and toil and hunger, and as well
The looming horrors of the far unknown.

Abe Givets heard the talk of salt and said
Nothing to anyone, but watched his chance
And sometimes went alone to the big hole.
He had a gnawing fear someone would find
That silver secret in the hidden dark,
And always watched that way from where he was
Or went where he could see there from the house.
Hearing one day a team upon the road
Where no teams passed, because this was the end,
He hurried to the house where he could see
The track that led to where his secret was.
He went into the woodshed where he could
Look down the road without his being seen —
As quiet as a cat that watches mice.
He saw the team come slowly up the hill,
Gus Warder's team and wearied with the pull,
And still a distance from his private track.
And through the door into the house he saw
Something that took his mind even from his salt.
He had left George to clear the barn and stack
Manure about the bottom of the house
To keep them warm against the winter wind,
While he himself went to the farthest shed
To oil his gear — a good full morning's work
And not one he'd be apt to interrupt

(84)

For anything but this suspicious watch
Now he saw he might indeed suspect
But not that anyone would take his salt;
This was a sight so unexpected to him
He hardly could take in just what it meant,
Not having thought that Ellen was a woman
Or anything but one to cook and wash,
And sometimes be a convenience to himself.
That anyone should want her, or that George —
Without a sound he drew himself away
And met Gus Warder as he stopped his team
Just at the track that led into the house,
Asking if Abe would lend his scaffolding
So he could mend his leaking cow-barn roof.

The teacher had no paper for her class,
What little was in town was valuable
And not for ABC. They used the slates
That had been almost out of use before,
And wrote upon the blackboard with what bits
Of softened stone and slate Miss Smith could find.
They liked it just as well. She kept the books
Locked up behind her desk, a precious hoard,
Passed out with care to those who read the best.
Oblivious though they were it seemed as if
The children felt responsibility,
As though they knew now in a special sense
They were the hope and prospect of the world.
They seemed to pay attention and discern

What things would aid them in existence here,
What things they must remember and pass on,
And drink them eagerly and ask for more.
There were no calls to lead them far away,
No cars to watch, no radio to hear,
No towns to see, and little enough to read.
So they were ready to forget the world
That once surrounded them, and face alone
Self-preservation in a wilderness.

v

The sun went southward in declining days.
The houses in the valley only saw
Six hours of sunshine in the best of skies.
The air was very cold, but still the snow
Waited beyond its long-accustomed time
And left the ground uncovered, rough and brown.
The children were distressed lest Christmas come
And find no snow to celebrate it with.
And even darker fears were in their minds;
Jack Warder after long and worrying thought
Said, 'Pa, I wonder about Santa Claus,
And if he's gone away like everything.
I wonder if we'll hang our stockings up
And if we do ——' He could not finish out
A thought so terrible. His father smiled.
'I don't believe that Santa Claus, my son,

Is much affected by this little change.
I guess he'll be around, about the same.'
   But Christmas, to be sure, could hardly be
The same as when a wagonload of toys,
Or nearly that, was purchased at the stores
In towns about, and brought to Saugersville
By parent hands as eager to give out
As little hands to take — when even the poor
Had some ten-cent-store toy, and not a child
But had some candy and a stick of gum.
So hands must set to work and make the best
That head and hands and few materials
Could manufacture for the Christmas tree.

John Herbert, who was quite a handy man,
And needed milk and eggs and maple sugar,
Devised a plan to suit this Christmas need.
With soft pine wood in plenty and his knife
He set to work to whittle animals,
And made a Noah's Ark as full of live
And antic creatures as there ever was.
Then, tiring of giraffes and elephants,
He made a farmyard and a barn as well
And needed only men to make it real.
This led him to the making of a doll,
And with a humor half-ironical
He carved a pretty girl so much like Gert
He sometimes thought she looked at him and laughed
Seeing her, done at last, upon his table,

(87)

Her naked body bright in fresh-cut wood,
He suddenly went hot, and turned away,
And made as though to put her in the fire.
But loving well the product of his hands
He threw a cover over her and thought,
'This lass must have some clothes. I'll find for her
Couturiers and milliners of style.'

Next day was lowering as though the sky
Was resting on the hills above the town.
He felt too near the ceiling of the clouds;
His heart was bursting out with restlessness
So after dinner (of potato soup
And bacon, and cabbage from his buried hoard)
He set out for a walk, stung by the cold
That cramped his hands within his tattered gloves.
The air was heavy and appalling still
As though it waited some unknown event.
He shivered as he walked, and felt again
The fear of hostile woods and walling hills
That slept behind the still security
Of day by day that dulled the sting of fear.
He went along the old cart track that led
Upon the hill's smooth crest, a stretch of land
Untenanted and bare of trees or brush,
A high and rolling sweep, a windy moor,
A down that crowned the ridge above the town
He saw the road below, the huddled stand
Of houses set about the small church spires,

The stone bulk of the mill, the tiny gleam —
The golden eagle on the flagpole top —
And quick and dark, the ever-flowing stream
He turned away, but to the north no hills
No blue and distant prospect of the world
To tell that even without men there was
A country not their own, another land;
No hills, no view, no other world at all,
But grey and heavy clouds that pressed around
As though they too were walls of wilderness
Impenetrable to foot as well as eye.
And here a panic fear assailed his mind,
A terror that was ignorant of what
Was terrible, a blind and sickening thing
That reason had no power to smother down.
He stumbled on, as though the rutted way
Could bring him out of panic into light
And he must hurry lest the devils gain.
And so like one beleaguered who descries
Across the plain the flag that brings relief,
He saw approaching him another one
Who fought the darkness of the heavy air
And walked in thought and maybe in despair.
  He saw it was a woman; soon he saw
May Warder's face that was an angel's face
That looks down into hell and knows the pain.
He drew a breath as though to live again,
Released from that dark pit he might have found
Because here was another living being

(89)

That looked out on the hills, the heavy clouds,
And faced with him the threat of doom and fear
They stood together in an air grown grey,
And for a moment's time that seemed as long
As all the months gone by since April first,
They said nothing at all. Above them now
As though this moment was the fated one
Long attended till these two were met
There came the silent messenger that fell
So still, so soft, so few, they saw it not
Until May felt upon her cheek its cold
And turned to him, just as he turned to her
To say the very words in the same breath —
'It's going to snow.' They laughed and felt their hearts
Rise up with joy as sudden as the snow.
Then suddenly the hill and all the field,
The town, the stream, the reaches of the road
Were gone behind the onslaught of the snow
That spread about them like a wall of fire.
They breathed the snow, their faces were beset,
Their eyes encrusted with the clinging flakes,
Their cheeks turned red with cold and pleasure in it.
'We'd better go,' said John. 'It's awfully thick.'
They bent their heads and pulled their collars up
Against the tickling fingers that crept in.
They could not talk, but walked the little road
Already covered with a scattered white
And soon to be obliterate entire.
Outside his house John stopped and said, 'Oh please,

I wish you would come in. I've something here —
I need some help. Come in, I'll show it to you.'
If there was hesitation, it was joy,
And there was none to see. May hastened in.
He shut the door behind. That first deep breath
They drew of warmth and shelter from the snow
Brought them together for a second's time
And made them one that sheltered against fear
And shut the door upon the wilderness.
It was as though someone had cast a stone
That disappeared within a darkened pool
But left a movement that betrayed its place.
May shook her clothes and held her hood and mitts
Before the fire that warmed the old black stove.
Her eyes were bright, for she at last was here.
John told her how he manufactured toys
And showed the Ark, the farmyard, and the dolls,
And drew at last his Gertrude from her shroud.
He thought the likeness was for him alone,
And if May saw it she did not remark,
But praised the pretty features and the joints
That moved the little limbs so gracefully.
'I'll make her lovely clothes,' she promised him,
'For Mother has a ragbag full of scraps
Will make her petticoats and hats and gowns —
I'll warrant you'll be proud of her.' He laughed.
'And if I sell her you will have your half.
We'd better go in business. We might make
Ten pounds of maple sugar or five cords

Of well-split wood, or anything else we need.'
They laughed together, and the warmth that spread
Throughout their bodies was a pleasant warmth
And not all generated by the stove.
The dark outside warned May she must get home.
She wrapped the doll inside her coat with care;
He saw her to the road and then turned back
And found his little house less lonely now.

VI

Lying awake in darkness by the side
Of one who slept and breathed so peacefully
She could have felt no guilt, nor did she feel,
Abe Givets planned what might the outcome be
Of this unlikely thing had come to pass.
He did not know how guilty George might be,
How long this matter had been going on,
What part his Ellen played, who seemed so still,
And had attacked him in this vulnerable
And wholly unpremeditated way.
Following his nature, which detested noise,
And thought a secret better than a scene,
He knew he would say nothing, since he knew
Not yet what he might say, if time should come
When something must be said, and said by him.
Meanwhile the old and never-healing sore
That marked his mind in that part where his 'rights'

Were placed, awoke again to bleed
And poison all his being with the fear
Lest he be cheated out of everything.

The snow grew deep, the children's hearts were glad,
And grown folks too found something in them rise
With pleasure at the brilliance all around.
The horses wore their bells, and men their boots,
A smell like Christmas seemed to fill the air.
The children in the school made toys of sticks
And painted them with what few paints they had.
'We'll have a Christmas party,' teacher said,
'And ask them all to come, yes everyone,
And have a tree, and presents if we can.
We'll plan it out so everything will be
As near to what it was as possible.'
She taught them songs and thought back lovingly
Of Christmas music and her radio.
There was an old victrola in the school
And thirty records that she knew by heart,
And could use only sparingly, for wear.
She thought, 'That music, all there was before,
Cannot just disappear and be no more.
It must be somewhere else now, singing still,
Though I can't hear it any more.' The tears
That came so easy to her pale blue eyes
Came now and blurred the room. She shook her
      head
And said, her voice a little sad but clear,

(93)

'We'll sing our carols over, now sing loud:
"Oh, little town of Bethlehem."''

By mid-December Grandma Smith was sure
The world was not worth living in. She said,
'Folks act so queer, they rile me most to death.
I don't care much for things the way they are,
And everyone deceitful. It was good
When I was young and God arranged things better.'
In vain the Reverend Yule urged resignation
And prayed with her, or rather by her side.
Her family had long since stopped arguing,
And could not interest her now in life.
Only to Roy, her favorite of her clan,
She spoke in words not wholly mutinous.
'I see there's changes, boy. You'll have to make
Your mark in Saugersville. The rest can go
Wherever these poor idiots say it's gone.
It doesn't matter anyway. The world
Is mostly right around a body's place
And doesn't need a radio to tell
You and your family what it thinks of you.
And even what the neighbors say don't matter
So long as you are strong enough to know
That what it says inside your head is right
And strong enough to listen and take heed.
For me, I've lived my share of life, and seen
This place spread out and now draw in again.
I haven't noticed folks at any time

(94)

Have differed much from any other time.
And everything comes out about the same.
I'm tired of it. I'll give you what I've got,
Although the money is no good to you,
At least not now. The land is pretty good.
You'd best get married, boy, and settle down.'
The old face smiled at him, the old eyes winked,
And for a moment an old twisted hand
Unused to give caresses, lay on his.
    It did not take her long to do her will.
Another week of slow disfranchisement,
Of sinking lower down than breath can stand
Or heart recover for another beat,
And she was still forever, peacefully.

Earl Backus bought the lovely wooden doll
For his lame Mildred, who was old for dolls
But loved them dearly for their company.
It was a darling creature; May had made
As pretty a wardrobe as a doll could ask.
John got his eggs and honey; for her share
May took some tea from Mrs. Backus' store,
Enough to brew a pot on Christmas Day.
    The Reverend Yule held church on Christmas Eve,
His little building all ablaze with lights.
(He had collected candles all the fall
Instead of pennies in the collection plate.)
And everybody came, or nearly so;
Not even Christmas in a frozen world

Would bring Abe Givets to church, though Ellen begged
With new-found bravery that she might go,
Till he said yes at last, with such a mouth
She was more frightened than if he'd said no.
But now she sat with eyes that shone with light,
The candles and the music in her heart,
The children like startled rabbits at her side.
But George was fast asleep at home; no thought
Of Ellen or of Christmas bothered him.
Save these, and others sick, or old, or young,
All Saugersville was there, as it had not
Spent Christmas Eve in church these many years.
The minister watched the faces that watched him,
And thought, 'We're doing well, they look awake.
The will of God works out in devious ways.'
He rose to pray: 'O God our Father, wise
And most benevolent, that blesses us
Although we know it not, give us to keep
Here in our hearts the memory of Christ,
Whose birth we celebrate now for the first
In our new world of loneliness and toil.
His story we will read and tell and love
That all may know that follow after here
The blessing that thou gave us in thy son.'
Jake Cramer listened with his head bent down,
And thought, 'This is the truth; it's up to us
To keep this thing alive. We mustn't forget.'
Earl Backus sighed a little to himself and thought,
'But this is just a little part of all

(96)

We must pass on. Our duty is so heavy
How can we ever do all that is right?'
Ede Salzenbach smoothed down her rabbit furs
She bought from Roy for half a box of shells
Left in the attic by her late deceased —
'Roy Smith could get his girl now if he would.'
May Warder listened with her heart so warm
It seemed as though the candles were all fires
That warmed her mind and made her glad and proud
And confident of all that lay ahead,
That she was strong, to bear the burden on.
John Herbert watched and did not close his eyes
And thought, 'She looks so good, so sweet, so true,
A part of these strong hills, and fit to live
And carry here a life that will be good.'
The organ played, they all stood up and sang,
The candles flickered, and the old man's hair
Shone silver in the pulpit. Like a cord
The music bound them all and made them strong:
'Oh come, all ye faithful, joyful and triumphant.'

The children found no lack on Christmas Day,
For there were toys enough, and Christmas trees
Hung with last Christmas' shining balls of glass,
And with some newer strings of cranberries
And popcorn white as snow; no lights of course,
But here and there a candle moulded small.
Treasures exchanged were tokens full of love,
For he who gave must spite himself to do it

And all were bought with dearer coin than money.
So even those who set most store by things,
Young girls, and women, and some men as well,
Were not ill pleased with what their Christmas brought,
And pride was added to the store of pride
Which lay already in the hearts of most
That things were going well in Saugersville
And fate was cheated — or at least so far.

But Christmas was not merry with the Munns,
Whose child was yet unborn, unwanted too,
And made them both as sad as though this were
Some strange calamity of unknown kind,
A part and parcel of the greater ill
That made a birth seem terrible and odd.
Robert watched his wife, who looked so thin,
The child a great excrescence on a frame
That hardly seemed to bear itself upright,
And always shook with tears and tears of fright.
On Christmas Day itself this fear came out
And stood bold in her eyes and on her face
And took voice in her mouth so that she cried
And fell upon her bed and clutched her hands —
'Oh Bob it is not time — it cannot be.
It lacks a month and more the way we count —
There's something wrong. Oh pain! Oh God — oh,
        Bob.'
Bob ran out to the road and looked and called;
Bill Countryman replied from the hotel.

'Quick, tell your wife. Get Mrs. Warder too.
I must get back. It's come a month too soon.'

It was a long and bitter day and night,
Mis' Warder tried to make a cheerful face
To face poor Robert with. But Bess screamed on
And nothing seemed of any help or good.
The women were as wise as they could be
With own experience, and old wives' tales,
And knew at least a little modern lore.
But Bess grew weaker and it seemed as though
She would not have the power to bear the babe.
They did all that they knew and asked advice.
The whole town helped with this, a town that leaned
With fierce anxiety about the bed
Of this their first-born child in their new world.
    At last, in morning light, the girl was born.
But Robert did not care. He sat close by
And watched the face that was too pale to live.
Mis' Warder in the kitchen wrung her hands.
'She bled so much — if anybody knew,
Or had the tools to give transfusion now,
Or maybe the right stimulant to give,
Or if — or if ——' She cried into her apron,
And there was none to answer or to help.
The tiny baby squalled; they wrapped it warm
And nursed it by the fire. Robert sat on,
Waiting for some faint sign, a look, a breath,
But knowing now that she would never stir

And never waken to his touch again.
They led him out at last. The Reverend Yule
Spoke gently to him as he passed, and went —
Beneath ecclesiastic calm the old
And burning tumult rising once again.
'She did not need to die, nor would have died
Had Schuylers Falls and its great hospital
And doctors, anaesthetics, and new blood
Remained to us, to us that need it so,
Being so frail, and ill equipped to keep
Our race continuing upon its earth.
Are we to be stripped naked to the cold
And primitive malevolence of earth
Just as we make an armor strong against
The force that fights so hard to keep us down,
Using for its tools our feeble bodies?'
He checked himself, that thought so wildly now,
So little like a minister of God.
But God seemed far away. The woman's screams
That yet were in his ears spoke older tongues
And made him tremble at the earth he walked.

And so with Dick Van Snell, and Grandma Smith,
Who both had wished to go nor felt regret,
They put the young and unsuccessful mother
That would have stayed had she had help enough
But by herself lacked the essential strength
To live and make life in a harder world.
The baby lived. The Warders took it home

And fed it drops of milk and water till
It lost its peaked look and tried to grow.
But Robert would not talk or even eat
Except as he was made to by his friends,
Not able even to think that Bess was gone,
But dull with anger at the burning thought,
'She might have lived; she might have still been here.'

As though Bess' death were signal to a fate
That waited to torment them, though it kept
Its final doom a secret in the hills,
Now sickness came upon them, young and old.
A cold, a fever, chills and aching pain,
A shattering weakness deep in blood and bone —
These bore them down like grain beneath the hail.
The clear and shining cold dissolved in rain,
The 'January thaw' brought mist and warmth
That made a body sick to feel the air
So wet, and sickly soft, and always grey.
In every house someone was sick, and some
Had more in bed than on their feet to nurse.
There were few remedies to give the sick
And only home-made doctors to attend.
What kind of thing it was they did not know,
Some bitter influenza, or a grippe,
That brought a terror with it worse than chills,
A terror justified. John Backus died,
A man they could not spare, both strong and wise,
And clever in the woods, a hunting man,

And hunting men were now again become
Leaders and providers to their town.
And then Jake Cramer's wife, who worked so hard
That there was nothing left, when she was ill,
To fight the sickness with; at last were still
The hands that never rested from the broom
That made her house a shining piece of glass
And kept her men in terror of their lives.
The youngest Countryman, a little boy,
Departed too. These three were all, and then
The plague diminished, and they hoped was gone.

May Warder was not sick, but worked so hard
She glimmered like a ghost before it went.
She went where she could be most help; one week
She spent at Winterhaus', where all were sick
Except Eugene, who kept the fires alight
And washed the pots and even the dirty sheets,
While May looked after everyone, alone.
Gert was the worst. The sickness took her bad
As though it meant to kill her if it could.
But May fought back and did the best she knew,
Watching the pretty face, so ugly now,
That once she hated worse than death itself.
And now thought only, 'Is she cooler now?
She must not die. I will not let her die.'
It was a struggle that allowed no time
For any thought except of life and death,
And May would think of nothing but of life.

Sometimes in fever Gert would cry out, 'John!'
And mutter words that did not make much sense,
And May had not the time to think of them,
Though sometimes she would hold her breath upon
The name that sounded like a call to her.
She won the fight, and beat not only death
But Gert's harsh cold reserve, that had been like
A wall between them since they were grown up.
She left the house, when they could tend themselves,
More nearly like a friend than Gert had had
Among her sex in all her selfish life.

While Gert was sick, Roy Smith had come to ask
Each day of May how things were going with her,
Until he too fell sick and in his fever
Raved on about her till his mother wept,
And made his father in anxiety swear.
'God damn the boy!' he cried. 'He must get well
And bed the girl to get her off his mind.'

John Herbert was not sick; he lent a hand
Wherever he could help. He carried wood,
And carried a corpse as well, when Backus died,
And tended cattle where the men were sick
And served as errand boy and handy man.
The ground below the mud was frozen hard,
They put the dead into the little vault —
A chancy thing, no undertaker there —
Though John suggested that they make a pyre

And burn the bodies as a safer course.
But such cremation would not do at all
To minds unmindful of ancestral rites
And busied only with the decent thing.

Earl Backus pondered on the many deaths —
For four were many of two hundred souls —
And he was shadowed by his brother's death
Who had been always with him, fifty years.
'The sickness, yes, they might have died the same,
If we'd had doctors and the hospital,
For people died of flu — whatever it was —
With every kind of medicine and help.
But Bess — she did not need to die. It's bad
If women can't have babies nowadays —
We must have babies here to carry on.
But then I guess we can. Poor Bess was weak;
She did not have much guts to do it with.
And there are others here could do it, sure.'
He thought of May, and Gert, and other girls
That looked as though they could have babies well
Without a doctor or a hospital.
'We must be careful, though, and all keep well.
We can't let sickness get a foothold here
Like this thing did. We shouldn't ketch diseases,
Not having traffic with the outside world.'
He grinned now to himself, but still his thoughts
Were trying always to plan out the way
The little group could live. No grief of his

Could darken wholly his ambitious mind
That looked forever to the future time.
The year had shown, until this date at least,
That they could winter over comfortably
On all that they had raised, with what they had
Left over from the richer times before.
No diet was as full, no food as good
As what they used to have. But no one starved
Or even hungered, and the cattle fed
Sufficiently from granary and loft.
He could not see but what another year,
Although their stores were gone, they would know more
About their needs and could again do well,
Providing providence provided rain
And sun enough to make their plantings grow.
Their clothes would wear, their houses need repair,
But there were deer for leather coats, and trees
That waited to be cut and sawed and planed.
Their greatest lack was sheep. They had no wool.
And salt — what would they do for that?
He brooded over these until at last
The greater question clouded over the less:
'What will become of us? We seem to be
The only human beings left alive.
If there are ever going to be again
Races of men, and cities, governments, —
At least upon this continent, like us,
Americans, — we are their fathers now,
And they depend on us and what we bring.

I do not think this can be really so.
There must be other villages alive.
One day we will discover them, they **us**,
And meeting fall to talking of a day
When we were all so near we did not care
Who lived or died or what became of us,
Too sure of everything — heat, light and power
And public education and the roads, —
Too little parts of a machine too great
For us to understand, or anyone,
So that we blamed ourselves no more at all
For anything that happened — that was bad;
I guess we took some credit for the good —
Complaining always of the government
Or capital, or labor, or the weather.
The last is all we can complain of now
With no one to account for but ourselves,
And near enough to see where blame is due,
If blame there is where everyone works hard
And does his best to keep himself alive.'
He chewed upon his empty pipe that now
Had smoked away his carefully guarded hoard
And stayed from habit only in his mouth.
('Next summer I must look out in the woods
For that wild plant that's something like tobacco.)
There's nothing I can find the answer to
By worrying on the future. Let it come.
We've not done bad so far. We'll just keep on.
I wish that John were here to help us go.'

III

☆

I

Because the need of salt was dominant,
And people now as well as stock were sick
To get a taste of it, that could not eat
Without these little grains to fill the blood,
Abe Givets meant to tell the Safety Board.
He had spent days and nights in planning this,
In thinking what to do, to get the most
Of his most lucky find. He cared for law
So much himself he felt all-powerful
Because by law he owned the stuff. He thought
Of all that he could get for it — enough
To keep him idle for a year at least
With produce, labor, all exchanged for salt.
But then he thought, 'The money is the best.
Some time, somewhere, the dollars will be good.
And if I take it now, when it is worth
Nothing to them, they'll give me more for salt
And then, when it is good, I will be rich.'
He brooded over this, and found it wise.
'Tomorrow I will tell, and they will pay.'

But sickness came upon him in the night;
He was the last to take it, who had said,
'My hide's too thick to ketch a bug like that.'
His Ellen nursed him with distaste but care,

(107)

And he was very sick and raving too.
And talked incessantly of something hid,
And then of salt and then he said, 'Be still.'
She did not listen. George was in her mind
And in her heart as well, and in her house.
He slept there now to do the chores and keep
A watch on things, but most of all a watch
On her whom he desired. The second night
Beside Abe's bed, where she had sat so long,
She looked upon the gnarled and working face,
The mouth that twisted down and muttered still,
The eyes that shut or open seemed to stare
Into her own that shrank to look at them.
He seemed more quiet now. She left her chair
And with no looking back went swiftly out
And shut the door and leaned her back upon it.
Her heart replied so loud to what she thought
She could not hear a sound. At last she knew
There was no sound behind her, nor above
Where in their beds the children were asleep.
Unthinking now, but answering her heart
She crept downstairs and into the back room.
George lay in darkness there but not asleep.

At some hour in the night the fever grew
And Abe flung restlessly about the bed
Talking of salt and riches and men's rights
Until at last he thought he must get up
To go and guard his valuable find.

He heard them crying for it, calling him,
And bringing wads of money in their hands.
Somehow he struggled up, put on his pants,
But could not find his shoes. He went without,
And like the ghost of an unburied man
Slipped down the stairs and out into the snow.
The cold came in upon him like a wind;
He did not feel it nor his naked feet.
It gave him strength but could not clear his mind;
Hot with intent he ran across the field.

Behind, the unlatched door swung open wide,
The cold blew in the house and banged the door
Where George and Ellen slept. She stirred and waked,
Then slid out of the bed and shut the door.
She crept upstairs and went into the room
Where on the chest the candle flickered still.
She called out 'Abe' and looked all round the room,
Then ran downstairs, the candle in her hand.
She looked into the privy; nothing there.
And then she saw the footsteps in the snow.
It seemed an hour before she could wake George
And make him understand that Abe was gone.
At last he was awake, and dressed, while she
Pulled on a coat and boots and followed him,
His lantern shining feeble in the night.
Across the field the naked footsteps went
And they hard after them. At last they came
To where the brush grew round the hidden hole —

And there upon his knees, deep in the snow,
Abe Givets reached with eager freezing hands
To fasten his rope ladder to the tree,
Avid to descend to opulence.
George came up to him suddenly. He screamed,
A wild inhuman sound, and staggered up.
George held the lantern up and spoke to him,
Trying to tell him to come back to bed
And showing him his face that he might know
He was a friend and here was Ellen too.
But Abe screamed out again and leapt at George
Shouting such ugly words that both at once
Realized their love was not a secret to him.
The lantern fell as George put up his hands,
But Ellen snatched it up before it died
And had a light to see the battle by.
At first George tried to catch the sick man's hands
And bring him safely home; he knew him mad
From fever and the sickness in his blood.
But Abe fought on, so furious in his strength
That George for all his weight was beaten off
And could get nowhere near to capture him.
Almost beneath their feet the snow gave way
And showed the precipitous rim of the deep hole.
Abe would not draw back but stood his ground,
Behind his back his precious hidden salt.
Ellen, who shivered in her nightgown, cold
With more than wind and snow, so strange a sight
So fierce a novelty before her eyes,

Called out to Abe, 'Come home and get to bed.
Oh can't you catch him George he's crazy wild.
Look out! The hole is close. Don't fall. Take care!'
George lumbered in again and reached for Abe,
Who fought more strongly back as though he saw
Now was his chance to kill, for wife and wealth.
He grabbed so tight of George, and pulled, and pushed,
That it was clear he meant to throw him down,
And Ellen screamed again, 'Oh George, watch out!'
The snow was trodden slippery underneath,
Where footing was not good at any time.
George with his boots was harder put to keep
A purchase on the snow until he could
Push back the madman to a safer spot.
He could not do it. Suddenly he fell.
Abe held him still but struggled to get clear.
They balanced on the edge; George half got up;
It seemed as though he could — then down again
And just as Ellen ran to grab them both
George went down backwards in the gaping hole
And with him Abe, who would not lose his hold.

So loud her heart was pounding in her ears
That Ellen could not hear, but felt the cries
Vibrating in the air, the crash of rock,
The shuffle and descent of muffling snow.
There was a moan, a cough, a rattle. The night
Was silent once again, and Ellen stood
Struck dumb and motionless, before she woke

And screamed, and called, and crept up to the edge
Her lantern in her hand. It was too dark,
And no one answered to her sobbing calls.

Earl Backus thought, when morning came again,
'There's something here besides a crazy fight
Between a man that's sick and one that's well.
Why did Abe go out in the field at night?
And where was Ellen then, and where was George?
Well, Abe is dead enough, and would have been
Without the fall, out in the snow at night
With fever in his blood. And as for George,
He's like to die. I guess he probably will,
Without a doctor or a way to find
Just where he's hurt inside, or what to do.
We ought to have an inquest held on Abe.
We've got to keep some sort of law a-going,
And there is something here that's mighty queer.'

George did not die, but lived to be a cripple
And Ellen's charge. The inquest which they held
When he was well enough to talk, though not
To walk and that he never was, absolved
All guilt, though there were heads that shook,
And tongues that wagged and ears that listened too
About the state of things at Givets' farm.
If there were sin in Ellen's artless love,
She saw that she would dearly pay for it

With George a useless and embittered man
Forever in his chair, forever cross;
Her husband he could be in proper time,
But worthless to her or to anyone.
The children helped her with the daily chores.
They lived somehow, and all the village helped,
Paying in kind for what they took of salt,
Abe's priceless treasure which was hid no more.
For those who found the bodies found the salt,
The ladder, and the place where Abe had dug.
Then Ellen remembered hearing Abe cry 'Salt!'
The Board of Safety cleared the spring and gave
A just division, ordering everyone
To pay the widow something that she needed.
So Ellen had a legacy of life
From him who figured only upon coin,
A currency of death, and death he had.

II

February brought such drifts of snow
That all the roads were filled and houses deep,
Half-buried in. The blue ascending smoke
Showed everywhere where people kept indoors
And only dug the small and difficult paths
To tend their stock or get the water in.
Now there was time to talk and time to think
Of these ten months which they had lived alone.

(113)

They counted over once again the goods
And evils which had come to them, and said,
'We've made out pretty well. We're mostly here.
There's sickness taken three, and childbirth one,
And one that died of just old age, and one
A suicide, and one an accident.
We can't be sure we mightn't have lost as many
In any year in which we had bad luck.
We've had enough to eat, we're warm enough.
The life is harder than it used to be,
But troubles are more real. We're thankful that
What's bad, or good, is right beneath your hand,
You know just where you're at, and what to do.
We're all of us more real, and more alive,
And Saugersville is real, more like a town,
And not a gas-pump on a concrete road.'

And there was time as well to make their plans,
Those Saturday night designs, so much discussed.
And now, with that assurance which the mind
Demands and manufactures if there's none,
Deciding they would live forever, they planned
To live as well as possible, as well
As in those other days — in which, alas,
They had spent little time in learning things
Would serve them well at such a time as this.
They had at least one man who understood
The whys and ways of electricity
And engines and machinery, a man

Born with the century and grown with it,
Along with twenty million other boys who made
Models of aeroplanes and wireless sets
When no one dreamt such things were any use.
Some natural understanding of their ways,
Some half-unknown affinity that told
The secrets that were strange to other men —
These made mechanics that were half inspired,
An essential product of a modern world.
Of these was Robert Munn, whose life was gone
With that machinery which made him live.
But now new plans, for steam, for electric power,
Awakened him, who had been dead with grief,
Abandoned by his world and by his wife.
They made their plan to use the water power,
Their faithful creek whose water never failed,
And Robert went to work and drew his plans
To see if he could make a dynamo.

And others with Gus Warder planned the crops.
In fact so many schemes were set afoot
The Board of Safety set a day each week
When everyone could meet and help discuss
The values of their schemes, and make new ones
And so devise a master plan for all.
Such meetings were not lacking fire and heat,
Embittered argument and sharp retort,
But Backus kept the fights within some bounds,
And finally emerged their plan for life
Their plan for Saugersville and for themselves.

With careful certainty the sun returned;
The valley days were longer; on the hills
The west was light till after five o'clock.
The brilliance of the February snow
That heartened everyone with double sun
Was kept intact by long-continued cold.
John Herbert found his skis that had been used
Not yet this winter — so much work to do
For others and himself, he had no time.
But now he waxed them well, and tightened straps
And set forth on the hills light-shod to fly.
The light had wakened so intense a scene
The eye could hardly bear the unending snow,
The purple distance, the staggering shadow blue,
The green of hemlocks in the surrounding woods.
He climbed, he turned, he sped down sloping fields,
With fences covered deep in drifts of snow
And nothing anywhere to stop his flight.
Here was a sudden strange intoxicant,
A wine of freedom and a song of change,
That set him suddenly apart from all
The labor and regret and loneliness.
His heart was opened out as though the wind
Enabled him to breathe new stronger air
And blew away the shadows in his head.
The sun burned down, the shining snow looked up,
And suddenly surrender made him king.
Denying any value to his life
He valued it too high, these months gone by,

Till now he saw at once it was no use
Unless it interwove with all that lay
Now clear before him, hills and trees and fields,
And in the valley far the smoke of fires.
The cold intoxicating air went deep
Into his lungs; he felt his heart grow big
And cried out suddenly across the snow
'I am alive and this is where I live.'
He thrust his poles deep in the snow and sped
Anew down shining fields. Across the hill
Beyond the buried valley and the trees,
He saw the red barns of the Warder farm,
And smiled, and cried out loud again for joy.

Their world was held within a frozen bowl
Of snowy earth and still and brilliant sky.
The cold kept all things motionless, the air
Was brittle and unyielding as a glass.
It seemed as though their fears were frozen up;
They felt themselves suspended in a world
So cold, so still, that it would never change.
Although the sun came northward day by day
The year's great wheel moved imperceptible
To bring again the anniversary.
'Maybe a year is all that's granted us,'
Earl Backus pondered with his restless mind,
Seeking forever answers where were none,
'And we'll be cast into the general doom
Upon the midnight of the end of March.

I doubt it though. I think our year s an earnest
We will go on in Saugersville a while.
And that's how we must live, to make the most
Of what we have as quickly as we can,
And plan to live at least a hundred years.
We know that we can live, so live we must.'

Then suddenly the end of winter came.
The drifts of snow caved in and sank right down
In little streams of water on the ground.
The creek broke out of ice and roared;
The wind blew riotous and wild all day
And shook the chimneys and the roofs at night.
Again the ground appeared, all dank and brown,
But bearing promise in its secret heart
Now running with the blood of winter springs.
The sun was burning hot and men came out
And turned their faces to its shining warmth
And felt the change of season in their limbs.

Coming upon May Warder in the woods,
Where she had gone not knowing any why
Except that it was spring, the sun was warm,
And she must wander and control her heart,
John Herbert took her hands and said at once,
'I think it's time we thought about our lives
And Saugersville and what the future is ——'
His eyes were laughing and his mouth looked warm.
She looked a question, but her heart was sure.

'We are the future of the world,' he said,
'And what we have we will perpetuate;
I think perhaps this is the finest place
God could have chosen, as maybe he chose,
To keep intact amid catastrophe.
We have the power, the strength, the will to live
Here all around us in these fields, this creek,
We can survive because we have the land.
I see it now. I see this is the best.
And you — you are my land, my "Newfoundland,"
And you and I will plow, and sow, and reap.'

They went together to the Reverend Yule,
Who smiled at them, and held May's hand, and touched
John's shoulder with a friendly tap, and said,
'Of course I will. We'll have it when you please.
I never made one would delight me more.
I think that there is hope for Saugersville,
A future in young hands. For yesterday
Roy Smith and Gertrude Winterhaus were here
To make the same request which you have made.'

As though remorseful for the bitter cold
Which held so long, the year now suddenly
Broke into spring a month ahead of time.
The snow went down the creek so rapidly
It seemed as though the earth had shed its coat
All in one hasty shrug. The ground lay warm

(119)

And sweet and soaking in the unclouded sun.
As though their hearts were equally unbound
The people stepped abroad and smiled and spoke
As though they knew their remnant of a world
Had better weather than it used to have,
And from now on the sun would be more bright,
The land more rich, the rain more plentiful,
And they, the last and desperate garrison,
More fortunate than any men before.
Sensing this deepening coursing of the blood,
This now enhanced, communal enterprise,
Earl with his wisdom which had not yet failed
Suggested they should hold a meeting soon,
A supper, and a dance, come one, come all.
And feeling something now within his heart
Said to the Board that planned this jubilee,
'I think that we should have it April first.'
He went that night to May and said to her,
'We're having a party on the first of April;
We want to celebrate our year's success.
Why don't you have your wedding on that day
And Gert and Roy as well? I don't know how
We could do better than to celebrate
Two weddings on that day, our New Year's Day.'
The girls said yes, the boys agreed as well,
Although John Herbert smiled a little smile
That was not wholly pleasant at the thought
That he and Gertrude should be married at once,
'To make,' he said, 'a Roman holiday.'

There was not much to eat left in the town.
There were potatoes, which began to sprout;
The apples and the cabbages were gone,
And turnips rotten, and the flour was low.
But there was corn in plenty for cornmeal,
And chickens still, though they were old and tough
And more were killed than should have been for eggs.
And there was milk, and sometimes meat as well,
A cow that had outlived her usefulness,
Or still a ham hung in the woodhouse roof,
And always there was game out in the woods.
Now that the green was showing in the gulfs,
A leaf of cowslip in a marshy spot,
They did not fear starvation, though they knew
They might be hungry before harvest time.

Though there was small complaint of government
Now that the Board had brought them through a year
With all the care and foresight that might be,
Their chairman now reminded them that law
Demanded new election now and then.
'What law?' they said, having forgotten law,
Being themselves the law in Saugersville.
'American law,' Earl Backus said. 'You know
We didn't use to think much of the law,
Being bothered out of mind with legislators.
The country was quite overcome with law,
There were too many, and yet not enough,
Until we were in doubt which was the best —

To scrap them all, or make a whole new batch.'
He laughed. 'And then they were all scrapped for us.
We didn't have to raise a hand. But now
We must think back to those beginning laws
Which aimed for justice in a place like this,
The few and simple rules of government
That were enough for small American towns
In days before there were so many towns,
So many people and so many miles
The only answer seemed so many laws.
And one of those ideas, original
To groups of men like us, is that
Each one must have his turn at government —
Or each that others want and will elect
We'll have election on the very day
We held it last, I think the third of April,
And everyone will vote for the new Board.'

Beside the old mill-dam a heap of stone
And new-cut logs lay ready for the time,
High water past, they could build up a dam
Big enough to make electric power.
In his garage, long quiet and shut up,
Now Robert labored to make power a fact,
Hindered and aided both at once by boys
Eager to learn, who saw in him their guide.
'We could have automobiles that run by steam,'
One said, 'There used to be such things, I know.'
'And we'll have tractors too, and all the things

They used to have before the power went off.'
Already in their minds a year had pushed
All previous time away, apart from them.
Their world was taken for granted without thought.
But Robert smiled, who knew how many things
Were lacking to the plans they planned so free.
Yet even he, his hands at work again
Providing some remittance of his grief
In hard construction in a makeshift scheme,
Felt how his heart was eager, how his mind
Concocted plans at least as bold as theirs.

Gus Warder looked out over muddy fields
That were already drying in the sun
And would be fit to plow and harrow and sow
Before many weeks were gone. He turned again
Within his mind the plan of crops and stock
He had worked out in winter with the Board,
That all might have enough of everything
And seed to spare, and cattle growing fat.
It could be done. The land was rich and deep,
And there were men to work that would work hard,
Their minds no longer on a wage or loan
But always at their backs a fierce demand,
A more insistent pressure, knowing well
How fine the line had grown that kept apart
The living and the dead, the dead who starved.
It would be difficult, this working out
Of independent living. This past year

They had been carried by the year before
And all the sane and reasonable years
They'd known before this mad unreason came.
It would be difficult. But given sun
And rain enough, no late or early frosts,
The sweat of every back that could be bent,
They would succeed. Gus folded over his arms
And dug his feet more deeply in the earth.
This was his kingdom and he would succeed.

Behind him in the house May's mother sat
And sewed and sewed upon the wedding dress,
The silver shining silk long put away,
A gift to her herself when she was young,
And never used, and now made up for May
The scanty dinner cooked upon the stove;
The sun shone in on the geraniums;
Ma Warder smiled, and rocked her squeaky chair.

III

The thirty-first of March was like a day
Two months ahead of time. The snow was gone,
And even here and there the grass was green.
That cold and bitter day a year ago
With snow still deep along the snow-fences,
And chilly air, and summer far away.

Was like a memory of winter's cold,
The shadow that was real but now is gone.
And all the day, as everyone worked hard
In preparation for tomorrow's feast,
The bright encircling sun that lighted up
The village with a soft and generous warmth
Seemed to find answer in new-warming hearts.
'There won't be many fancy things to eat,'
Said Maria Winterhaus, bent over her stove,
Concocting dainties out of anything;
'But we'll all do our part to see there's lots
Of such plain food as folks has got to give.'

Young Roy had shot a deer, some partridge too,
Poor skinny things, but would be savory,
When well cooked up with herbs and butter fat.
Fast-hoarded stores of things not eaten now —
White sugar, and some chocolate, and a can
Of grapefruit and a box of apricots —
Were brought from secret shelves for this great day.
May Warder tried her dress for the last time,
Her mother worrying round it like a hen.
The shining silk was a soft benison,
A blessing to the lovely warming face
That never looked so pretty or so bright.
And in her house the other bride as well
Worked on a wedding dress, which once had been
The gayest at the River City Ball,
And now with decorous changes would suffice

To deck her at the altar. This girl too
Had shining eyes, that while she answered back
In petulant voice her mother's platitudes
Showed something deep and happy in her heart

John Herbert brushed his one good suit of clothes
And whistled to himself. He had worked hard
To make his little house fit for his May;
He'd had Mis' Countryman come in to clean.
The windows shone like ice. The stove was blacked,
The floors were white, and on the mantel shelf
His two brass candlesticks were bright as gold.
'She'll fix it as she likes,' he thought; 'two rooms
Is not so very much; but we could make
The attic livable with dormers there,
Or even build an ell out to the west.'
His mind looked far ahead, and in the haze
Which his warm heart engendered now he saw
A family at his hearth, himself the head.
Like some old picture in an antique frame
He saw the children at his knee, his wife
Knitting across from him, her face bent down
Smiling in secret happiness. And he,
The teacher and protector of his flock,
Read to them from a book, the firelight bright
On small attentive heads and on the wall
Where hung behind him his old hunting gun.
John shook himself and laughed and thought again,
'There's something to it, though. We're back to that.'

Ede Salzenbach took out her taffeta dress,
Her uniform for funerals and weddings,
And smoothed its pleats and thought, 'This is the
    last.
There'll be no clothes like this for anyone
In years to come. We'll all go dressed in hides.'
She grinned at thinking how some folks she knew
Would look dressed up in skins. Her eager mind,
Which had fed always on things close at hand
And knew no larger world, was not dismayed
So long as there was gossip to be had,
And there was gossip while folks lived at all.
Now prospect of two weddings and a feast
Was more than wealth to her; her eyes were bright.
'Of course it's not so comfortable a life,
But folks don't get away. They're all right here,
And I can see them from my kitchen door.'

Lighting his candle with a splinter's end
The Reverend Yule sat down to his plain meal,
Watching across the table to the west
Where only now the last clear light declined.
The western hill rose upward like a wall,
Its battlement the interlocking trees
Which seemed already thick with spring's advance.
'The light lasts late,' he thought, 'but night will
    come,
The very night of March that brought us woe.
One year gone by. A year — so little time

In even human life, and in God's sight
A breath, a heart beat, or a drop of rain.'
He ate his smoky meat, and drank his milk.
'There must be other men. I think there are,
But isolated too. Some day we'll meet;
But for the time, and maybe even then,
We are the ones to carry knowledge on.
We are the messengers must bear the weight
Of even more than we can understand.'
He shook his head. 'There does not seem much
        chance
Of keeping anything but here and there
A principle, an old long-tested truth
We can pass on to others like a light
To help in darkness which must now be more
Than ever darkness to men's feeble lights.'
He pushed away his plate, and covering his face
He prayed the stillest and most fervent prayer
That any man can pray, that he be strong
And do his part and more and may not fail.
'It may be we were given this very fate
That we may see thee better. God,' he prayed,
'Now let me know thee more, inspire my heart
With strength not just to bear but to lead on
That men who have heard once of thee may know
They too must tell thy strength, so that the day
May never come when our descendants turn
And look with questioning eyes and ask again,
"Christ Jesus? Who was he? What did he do?"

The night fell sweetly on the little town
Deep in its hills that breathed like cows asleep
The fragrant odors of the earth. The creek
Rushed down into the valley with a sound
Loud and full-throated; of its score of falls,
Each with a private song, it made a chord
That sounded like an organ in the night.
Earl Backus stood upon the bridge. The sound
Pressed in and out upon his ears until
He did not know which beat the steadiest,
The water or his blood. 'They are the same,
For I am of that creek and it of me.
We are but different parts of the same thing.'
The air was good. He breathed it deep. His heart
Beat strongly in his chest. He clenched his hands
Upon the bridge rail, looked into the night.
'Another hour, and all our year is spent.
The time has come full circle. Oh a year,
It's nothing but a measurement of man.
And this has been the longest of our years.
Maybe the shortest. It may be the last,
If God keeps anniversaries, and likes
To do things on the proper date again.
Maybe at midnight then, upon the hour
As when John Herbert saw his light go dim,
We will depart upon as blind a road

As took all we had known, a year ago.
It seems as though the end at least was quick,
Unless our time is all balled up, and years
And centuries can happen in between
Midnight and midnight-one. It may be so.'
He drew so deep a sigh his throat swelled up.
His hands unclenched and dropped. He turned away
And paced the road. There were few lights that showed,
For folks were mostly all abed, tired out
Preparing for the party, sleeping deep
In preparation for a gay night's work.
'We have done well so far. That'll give us strength
To keep on doing well. I hope we can,
But there's more work here than we half conceive,
And every year will be a fight to live,
Just to survive. That's why it will be hard
To keep and to pass on the best we have,
Those things of our old world which should go on,
Showing that men have lived so many years,
So many thousand years, and learned a few,
A very few directions for the way.
I think perhaps we cannot do this thing;
Our children's children will start to forget
And from then on they will descend again
The path that once they worked so hard to climb.
I see them dressed in furs, and living here
Along this stream, where in the grass and weeds
A few old stones will be our Saugersville.'
He shook his head. 'I think that this may be.

(130)

I hope that it will not. I'll do my best,
And I am strong, and most of us are strong.
If we get by this fatal hour tonight,
We will keep on, and be the human race.'

John Herbert was still working in his house,
Burning his candles at a reckless rate,
Thinking, 'We'll have no need of them tomorrow;
Our darkness will be sweeter than my light.'
He banked his fire and swept the ashes up,
Conscious of night that pressed upon the panes
A dark and maybe hostile world outside.
He looked into the brilliant coals of wood
And saw in them his city and her towers,
And thought of lights and noise and multitudes
He would not see again. His chest grew tight
And for a moment in his heart he wept,
Feeling his sorrow gnaw him once again.
But that departed and he thought of May
And of the life that now came forward, fair
With smiling face, and hands stretched out to him.
He blew out all his lights but one, and said,
Looking into the flame that burned so clear,
'The time has come again. The year is gone.
I do not think my candle will fade out.
We have come closer to the heart of things.
Maybe' — he laughed, and looked out to the night —
'Maybe instead we'll see our lights come on.
Maybe at midnight will our world return,

And all this year become a moment's dream
Which I and others, perhaps only I,
Have dreamed in some few seconds of one night.
And at that hour, when power flows on in lines
Not ever really empty, and below
I hear upon the road the trucks go by,
I will forget, we'll all forget this year
That was a moment's dream of something real.'
He stood as still as though he were all thought,
Knowing for one that he was better now
Than on that night a year gone by, more strong
More able to take hold of life, and joy.
'Maybe,' he said again, and shrugged and grinned
And started now for bed. He wound his watch
And saw the hands move slowly onward toward
The midnight of the thirty-first of March.